EYES OF THE INTRUDER . . .

There was another roll of distant thunder, another flash of silver light, causing me to remind myself I wasn't afraid of storms. The rain was definitely slackening now.

I went to the window to check. It was impossible to tell, with so many rivulets racing down the pane. I leaned closer, and froze in that posture, staring, praying I was imagining it—that pair of eyes, not my own. A white moon of a face floated in space, there at the window, just about level with mine. It was too dark to discern fine details. Black hair, a slash of shadow across the eyes— then it was gone.

My screams bounced off the walls, reverberated, rang. My first rational thought was of escape. My second was that to escape, I'd have to go out that menacing door, where he was. Probably waiting for me with an ax in his hand. Guns were too civilized for this wilderness . . .

THE POLKA DOT NUDE

JOAN SMITH

JOVE BOOKS, NEW YORK

THE POLKA DOT NUDE

A Jove Book / published by arrangement with
the author

PRINTING HISTORY
Jove edition / February 1989

ISBN: 0-515-09753-5

Jove Books are published by The Berkley Publishing Group,
200 Madison Avenue, New York, New York 10016.
The name "JOVE" and the "J" logo
are trademarks belonging to Jove Publications, Inc.

PRINTED IN THE UNITED STATES OF AMERICA

10 9 8 7 6 5 4 3 2 1

CHAPTER 1

Good luck is a relative stranger to me, but there happened to be a nail driven into the wall at the spot where I wanted to hang Rosalie's painting. I lifted the picture and jiggled the wire of the big gilt frame till the picture hung straight, then stood back to assess the effect. It really was a beautiful painting. The style, Rosalie told me, was called "pointillism," a painstaking refinement on impressionism, with every brushstroke forming a round dot, like confetti. A painter would have to be a masochist to adopt such a style, which probably accounts for the rarity of these pointillist works.

From across the room, the individual daubs of pigment merged to form the nude body of a young woman. She stood with her back to the viewer, peering over her shoulder. The sun struck her from the left, bathing that side in dappled light. The pigments—small, perfect dots of pink, orange, and gold—coalesced to a shimmering opal. The right side, away from the sun, was done in blue, green, and purple. The two shadings blended to an indeterminate shadow down the middle of the spine. Coppery hair, bright as the sun, was twisted into a knot, with tendrils falling along the legendary face of Rosalie Hart. She looked half-child, half-wanton, and all female.

Rosalie gave the picture to me when I spent a week with her last month. I treasured it not only for its beauty, but because of Rosalie. She had painted this self-portrait from a photograph. "They say you're not supposed to paint from pictures, but lots of them did it that way," she assured me. "Many's the time I've seen Utrillo sorting through post-cards at a kiosk in France, to pick out his next painting, and now he's hanging in the Louvre."

She had often mingled with the artists in France during her frequent holidays there. The famous names sprinkled on her conversation had the aroma of history for me. I smiled fondly at the picture, remembering my sojourn with Rosalie. Rosalie Hart—sweetheart of silver screen, a real honest-to-God legend in her own time. And I, Audrey Dane, was the person chosen to write her biography. We hadn't a thing in common, yet we'd got on famously. Or maybe she just liked having an audience again, someone to pay undivided attention to her. "I want the gal who did Bunnie Winters," Rosalie had said. Bunnie had been her main competition in movies fifty years before. "If Dane can make Bunnie's dull life readable, she'll make a best-seller of mine."

Certainly the ingredients were all there. Rosalie had seen it all, done it all, and kept copious records in the way of letters, journals, and photographs. The woman was part pack rat. Rosalie was only a little younger than the century. She'd broken into films when she was fifteen and grown up with the industry, making the transition from silents to talkies without a hitch. Her sweet, cooing little voice had turned querulous with age by the time I met her. Half a dozen of her movies still played at film festivals around the country.

Her work hadn't kept her from a lively personal life,

either. Into it she'd squeezed five husbands and more lovers than even she, with all her letters and diaries, could keep track of. There were rumors of an illegitimate child of unknown paternity as well.

Rosalie had been coy about that. "We won't tell it all. I may do a sequel, if it takes." She laughed slyly. I figured that if there *had* been a child, it was born late in her life, after her retirement. She'd been drinking heavily in her forties, and gone to a European clinic for a year or so to dry out. Her beauty had faded by then, and her comeback attempt wasn't successful.

Beauty wasn't a word anyone would associate with the egocentric, dotty woman I'd interviewed in California. Her face looked like a skull with a crumpled sheet of yellow plastic pulled over it, but the old films and photographs showed what she once had been. So did the painting. There was a reckless, renegade smile lurking at the corners of her lips and lighting her eyes. They didn't make them like Rosalie anymore. Of course, it's hard to be a rebel when everything's permitted.

What Rosalie rebelled against these days was age and obscurity. She lived in one wing of a ramshackle mansion called Hartland. All but one wing was boarded up. The famous rose gardens were gone to weed, the white paint peeling. It looked so sad, like an antebellum mansion, after the war. Her only companion was her old friend and stand-in, Lorraine Taylor. They'd been friends for decades, through the good times and the bad. There, amidst the decaying souvenirs, they relived the past, looking over cards and dried flowers from princes and presidents, exotic outfits left over from her ancient films, while a couple of Rolls-Royces turned to rust in the tumbledown garage cum stables.

But I had to shake off this nostalgic mood. The book

might end on a sad note; it had to start on an upbeat. I went to the table and glanced over the research material. The ink in the diaries and letters was fading. It hadn't photocopied well, so I was using the original documents, which made me nervous. I sat down in front of my brand-new typewriter with the shiny film ribbon. This book had to be good—it would have my name on it. Bunnie Winters' bio hadn't, but this time it would say "as told to Audrey Dane."

Just as I placed my fingers over the keyboard, a car pulled up next door. Through the window, I saw it was a white Mercedes. The door opened and a tall, dark-haired man got out. He went to Simcoe's cottage, knocked, and then disappeared through the door. The man didn't seem a likely tenant for the other cottage. Simcoe owned two besides his own house. The three clapboard buildings hugged the shore of the St. Lawrence River, with a magnificent view of the Thousand Islands beyond. The view was the sole attraction discovered so far. The actual cottages were run-down, furnished in decaying Sears-Roebuck, and not close to any big city. Privacy to write my book was what had brought me to this corner of the state, no matter what my friends and family thought. I wasn't here because of Garth. I'd been jilted by better men than Garth Schuyler, hadn't I? Oh, but there wasn't anyone better than Garth! I looked again at the man from the Mercedes. If my privacy had to be invaded by anybody, he wasn't a bad invader.

Never mind, I told myself firmly, you can enjoy an orgasm some other time. You're here to earn your advance, the one that paid for this new typewriter and the rent on the cottage. I centered the paper and typed "Chapter One." The new ribbon gave a sharp, clean outline to the letters. Looking at the length of it feed out from the cartridge, I could see the word *dog*, clearly legible. "The quick brown fox mumps over the lazy dog," I had written, to test that every letter worked perfectly. The *j* actually worked perfectly too, but my fingers didn't. If this new book made me rich, my next purchase would be a word processor.

The empty white sheet held no terrors for me. It was an invitation and a challenge. Long before dark, I had filled five sheets, outlining the geographical and social background of Elinor Brunn, who, along about chapter three, would metamorphose into Rosalie Hart.

A sharp rap at the door brought me back to the present. Simcoe here to point out some other splendor of this hovel, I thought, but through the front window the rear end of the Mercedes was seen, moved over to the other cottage now. Remembering the fantasy who drove it, I tucked my hair behind my ear, and regretted my lack of lipstick, and Dad's old checked shirt that hung loose over my jeans. A pair of moccasins with both toes in good repair would have been welcome too. When I opened the door to a vision who might have been Cary Grant's younger brother, I regretted all these lapses even more deeply.

"Hi, I'm your new neighbor. I just thought I'd drop over and introduce myself. I've hired the cottage next door," the man said. He was so tall he had to bend his head to see me.

Life, in case I haven't mentioned it before, has played a few mean tricks on me. I'm tall and angular, with a boyish figure. I don't mind the lack of hips and bosoms so much these days, but during my formative years it gave me a complex that I'm still working my way out of, because of Helen. I owe a lot of complexes to Helen. If Freud had ever known her, there'd be a Helen complex, right alongside of Oedipus and Electra. Helen's my older, perfectly gorgeous sister. She's smarter than I am, prettier, and much nicer—or so I thought, till she set her baby blues on Garth. All my teachers used to ask with surprised disappointment if I was *really* Helen Dane's sister. Even before I got miserable marks in math and science they used to ask. After just one look at my square, unlovely face, they couldn't credit I'd sprung from the same loins as Helen.

Helen, after breezing through Hunter with straight *A*'s, got a terrific job on the editorial staff of a women's magazine. Such tough assignments as covering fashion shows in Paris, and visiting the best holiday spots, were her lot. She invited Garth and me to go with her to Aspen last winter. Garth was interested in hot-dog skiing at the time, and as it turned out, Helen supplied the buns. They got married last month, and are presently in Greece on their honeymoon. If she weren't on her honeymoon, she'd probably come home married to a Greek shipping magnate. Garth is a dazzlingly handsome plastic surgeon who makes a fortune reconstructing ladies' faces. Helen won't even deteriorate with age. She'll just go on, gorgeous forever, having a nip here, a tuck there. Cary Grant's younger brother would love Helen.

But it's unfair to blame Fate and Helen for all my failings. It was my own fault that I now stood in rags before this vision in the impeccably clean sports shirt and light blue cords. He was the right age, too, somewhere around the middle thirties, to match my eight and twenty years. Pronounced grooves marked his forehead and the corners of his eyes, to give him his own unique look. Whoever thought such a mirage would visit me while I worked? Whoever dreamed he'd be a good six inches taller than me; that he'd have jet-black hair, my favorite color in men; eyes the shade of undiluted coffee; teeth that belonged in a toothpaste ad; and that he'd stand smiling, waiting to be invited into the shambles I'd created of an already bad room? Nobody could possibly have foreseen this unwelcome miracle, and it was therefore the fault of Fate, since I couldn't reasonably blame Helen.

"Hello, nice to meet you. I'm Audrey Dane," I said, and shook his hand.

"Brad O'Malley," he said, and gave my fingers a firm shake. Even his hands were gorgeous—tanned, strong, with a gold college ring on his finger.

"Please come in," I invited, with only lukewarm enthusiasm. He'd take me for a bag lady, living in squalor. "Don't mind the looks of the place. I've been working."

"Am I interrupting? Sorry—I won't stay a minute." The coffee eyes were already touring the shambles: the typewriter and the brown carton of research from which papers flowed over onto the table. There was no desk. I ate at one end of the table, worked at the other. A coffee cup, a crust of unfinished rye bread, and a heaped ashtray bore mute testimony to my slovenliness.

"Could I get you something to drink? A coffee—beer?"

"Beer would hit the spot, if it's no trouble."

For Cary Grant's brother, I'd have walked through live coals for anything his little heart desired. "It's no trouble."

I flew to the kitchen and got two nearly cold beers from the frig. The glasses, once the proud holders of peanut butter, were decorated with orange ducks, dressed in caps and sweaters. I took the bottles to the living room. Brad had risked his clean cords on the chintz sofa, but leapt up like a puppet on a string when I came in. So polite!

"I'm afraid these cottages don't come very well equipped," I apologized, and handed him the bottle.

"Privacy's the thing," he said forgivingly, then twisted the top and stood waiting for me to sit down. Decisions, decisions! Did I sit beside him on the sofa like a normal human being, or did I reveal my neuroticism and drag the chair from the table? I sat on the sofa, at the far end from him.

After a brief examination of the split toe of my mocassin, I said, "O'Malley, did you say your name is? That sounds Irish." A truly brilliant opening gambit. There was nowhere for this conversation to go but up.

"You're right, I am. Are you a teacher, Miss Dane?"

"Audrey! No, I don't teach. What made you think that?" Because you look like Miss Grundy, that's why.

"Who else has time to sequester herself in the woods for a summer? And you have the tools of the trade with you— books." He nodded toward the table, where a dictionary lay open.

I felt the first twinge of confidence since his arrival. "Actually, I'm a writer," I announced. A writer was a nice thing to be—interesting, different. Maybe even accounting for the bohemian style of self and accommodations? Helen had never written a book. Helen was too busy living one—a regular Harlequin Romance. People were usually surprised to hear I wrote. They didn't usually go into shock, however, as Brad O'Malley was doing.

"A writer! How interesting. Hey, this is a marvelous break for me." A smile as wide as Texas and as bright as sunshine bedazzled me. "Who are you? What do you write?" he pressed on eagerly.

"I'm Audrey Dane," I reminded him. The smile began to dwindle. He thought maybe I was Susan Sontag, Rosalie Wildewood?

"I mean what name do you write under?"

"My own. I'm a spook."

"A what?"

"A ghost-writer. You read *The Bunnie Winters Legend*?"

"I'm afraid I missed that one. Did you write any others?"

"Nothing you'd be familiar with." He wouldn't have

read *The Mystery at the Old Mill*, or *The Secret of Meadowvale*, my two preteen mysteries. I had failed to impress him. But in a flash I slipped another arrow into my bow. "I'm working on the life of Rosalie Hart at the moment," I said casually.

Another spasm of delighted shock possessed his face. "Rosalie Hart! No kidding! That should be a good one. I'll be looking forward to that. Have you actually met her?"

"Oh yes, I spent a week at Hartland. That's her home in California."

"I know. I'm a Hart fan."

"What do *you* do, Brad?" I asked. What I hoped to learn was why he said it was a marvelous break for him that I was a writer.

"I teach literature at a little college not too far from here. A private college."

"Oh." This came as a surprise. His appearance didn't suggest a little anything. Big-city doctor, lawyer, businessman—even actor—seemed more his style. My writer's eye garnered up jarring details. The few lecturers I knew didn't drive new Mercedes cars. Plastic surgeons like Garth Schuyler drove Mercedes cars. What was a lecturer doing in a hand-stitched shirt and Gucci loafers? Why did the watch on his wrist say Rolex, instead of Timex? Looking up suddenly from my examination of his watch, I noticed his eyes were narrowed, looking at me warily, as if suspicious, or afraid . . . of what? What threat could I possibly pose to Brad O'Malley?

"I do a bit of writing myself, on the side," he said quickly. "Publish or perish, you know. Nothing you'd have read," he added, a hint of condescension creeping into his tone. "I do academic writing. Modern poetry is my field."

When you're a writer, you're sensitive to people's actions and reactions as well as appearance. Brad was on the defense, and I hadn't attacked yet. "I love modern poetry," I said encouragingly.

"By modern poetry, I don't mean contemporary poetry," he pointed out. "The modern era in poetry begins at the time of World War I."

"I know. Yeats, Eliot, Auden—I love them all. Much better than the contemporary poets. Of course Hopkins precedes the usual date given. The father of them all, in my opinion," I added firmly. An inner wince stabbed me. I was doing it again, as if I were back in college, staking my claim to intellectual equality, and depressing any hope of romantic involvement in the process. Why couldn't I gush, like other women?

"Right. Naturally." He drained the bottle of beer and rose to that glorious height of six feet, two or three inches. In my moccasins, I hardly came to his neck. It wasn't often I could physically look up to a man. "It was nice to meet you, Audrey. We'll be bumping into each other from time to time, being neighbors."

I had a sinking feeling any meetings would be purely accidental. Gush, dammit! You don't learn to gush in two minutes. The voice that came out of my mouth was as cold as frost. "I'll be hunched over my typewriter most of the time." I could feel my damned eyebrow lift in that way that makes me look haughty.

He smiled easily—almost intimately. "I'll know where to find you then." It must be wonderful to be so full of yourself you didn't recognize a putdown when you heard one.

I made another stab at gushing. "Great. If you want to borrow anything, feel free to call. A cup of sugar, typewriter, dictionary . . ."

"I brought all those things with me. Bye." He smiled again and ducked his head out of the door.

Idiot! How long has it been since you met a man taller than you, with a job, and a clean shave and a car newer than 1970? A man who speaks real English, and gets his butt off the chair when you come into the room? Not since last June, when you met Garth Schuyler. But do you know enough to smile? No, you meet him at the door in dirty jeans and falling-apart slippers, and can't let him patronize you a little. You have to go dragging in Gerard Manley Hopkins. You couldn't name one poem Hopkins wrote. You hated Hopkins worse than Eliot. Helen was right: You shouldn't let your brains go to your head. You should detour them to your hormones; big sister knows best.

I went to the window and stood behind the curtains to watch him unpack his car. Beautiful matching bags. Vuitton luggage, for God's sake. A case of wine, more cartons than you'd think that little trunk could hold. A hi-fi, no TV. Records—probably Beethoven. The trunk of my own rusty Ford had come full of research, typewriter, TV, and one plaid soft-walled suitcase of clothes. I hadn't even brought a coffeepot, and I planned to survive largely on coffee. Luckily Simcoe's cottage came equipped with an antique aluminum pot, with a little glass bubble on top.

These feelings of inadequacy weren't good for me. I went back to the table and started to read over the five pages of *Queen of Hearts* written so far. That was the working title of Rosalie's book. I had about umpteen compound sentences in a row, and marked them for revision. When I looked at my watch, it was five o'clock. I had intended to call Bell about getting a phone installed, but Brad's visit put it out of my mind. An editor (or a handsome neighbor for that matter) couldn't call me if he wanted to. Nobody else would. The family were the only other ones who knew where I was.

The next thing to consider was food—whether to fry a

couple of eggs here or drive into town for a hamburger.
While I stood staring at the carton of eggs, there was a wrap
at the door, and Brad peeked his head in.

"Me again. Have you eaten?"

I was startled that he'd come back, and so soon. "No."

"Good—don't. I'm simmering a boeuf bourguignon. It
should be ready in a couple of hours. Why don't you come
over around six-thirty and we'll have a drink first?"

"A boeuf bourguigon?" I asked, bewildered.

"It's fast and easy." An egg was fast and easy. A steak
was possible; boeuf bourguignon was for restaurants. "I just
want to put a few things away and take a shower. I look
forward to seeing you at six-thirty."

"I'll be there. Thanks."

The black head vanished, and I put the eggs back in the
fridge. Boeuf bourguignon! He hadn't even *unpacked* yet
and he was simmering a French dish. Was this man real, or
was I dreaming him? "I bet he even does windows," I
muttered to myself, and grabbed an apple to sustain me till
dinnertime.

I decided to pop over and use Simcoe's phone to call
Bell. For some as-yet-undetermined reason, he was always
reluctant to let me inside his house. I thought maybe his
wife was a bit strange. She sat behind the curtains at the
window all day, peeking out. At the door, Simcoe said he'd
make the call for me, and let me know when Bell could
come.

"Thanks, Mr. Simcoe."

"You're very welcome. I guess you were pretty surprised
to see young O'Malley land in on you, eh, Miss Dane?" His
merry blue eyes danced behind a pair of glasses. Simcoe
was best described by what was missing. His glasses were
rimless, his head was hairless, and his mouth partially
toothless. He was a short, stocky man, who had worn the

same blue shirt and trousers and suspenders since the first time I saw him.

"I certainly was. You didn't mention renting the other cottage."

"I wanted to surprise you," he said, and laughed.

Simcoe was definitely not the kind of person to plan delightful surprises for his tenants, but I just said, "You succeeded."

"Oh I can keep a secret." He laughed again, and closed the door.

I went back to my own cottage, puzzling over that cryptic conversation. For some reason, it reminded me of the fleeting moment when I'd looked up and seen Brad narrowing his eyes at me. I shook the thought away. Neurotic, that's what I was. A silver cloud had chanced my way, and I wouldn't spoil it by looking for a lead lining. Ah, "The Leaden Echo and the Golden Echo"! Hopkins had written that one. Lousy poem.

CHAPTER 2

You could hardly wear jeans and moccasins to a dinner whose main course didn't even speak English. Sorting through my clothes, I decided unwrinkled white slacks were better than a rumpled skirt. The navy silk shirt was okay; the boring old gold chains worn with everything went with it as well. What bliss to slide into high-heeled sandals, knowing you wouldn't have to either buckle your knees or stoop, or else soar above your date's head. I have this theory that short men and tall women share a similar complex—like Napoleon's being an overachiever to compensate for being a little runt. There were lots of others too—Voltaire and the Marquis de Sade came to mind. And since women are supposed to be small, maybe we have to over-compensate if we're tall. If I could only think of a few tall female achievers . . .

The mirror in the bathroom was designed for Napoleon. I kicked off the sandals to consider renovations to my face. Some vestige of my mother's Slavic origins were still visible in my high, wide cheekbones and full lips, but the strain was diluted by her Anglo-Saxon spouse. I credit my straight nose and green eyes to Dad. People who didn't have

to contend with it admired my ruler-straight hair. I wouldn't
mind a wave or two myself, but the roller hasn't been
invented that can accomplish that miracle. At the moment,
a tawny mane hung in straight shocks down either side of
my face. I brushed it back and twirled it into a figure eight
on the back of my head.

I carefully applied a blusher and lipstick, then picked up
the eyebrow pencil. In an uncharacteristic fit of gullibility,
I had listened to a salesclerk who assured me this stick of
kohl would transform me into a beauty. Used by Cleopatra,
she said. I wondered how tall Cleopatra had been. Cleo had
obviously known something I didn't. The kohl crumbled
and smudged, and made me look as if I'd caught my head
in a chimney. I wiped till only a suggestion of smoke clung
to the base of my lashes. After the red from rubbing had
faded, I stuffed a fresh pack of cigarettes into my purse, put
my sandals on, and was off.

"I'm glad you decided to come casual. I meant to tell you
to," Brad said at his front door, where he met me a minute
later. He was done up in a white shirt and striped tie, navy
blazer and fawn trousers himself, and looked about as
casual as an engraved invitation to the White House.

My senses were assaulted on all sides as I went into the
dimly lit cottage. Strange discordant music issued from the
stereo. There was a wail of violins carrying the melody,
enriched below by breathy woodwinds, and the throb of
drums. It was an insinuating rhythm that obtruded on the
ear. An infernal racket might be a clearer description. The
spicy aroma of meat simmering in herbs and wine wafted on
the air, mingling with the music, but the greatest assault was
on the eyes.

I had seen this cottage myself two days ago. It had been
a dump, like my own. What had he done to it, to make it
look like a seraglio? The embroidered throw covering the

sofa vaguely suggested India. On it were tossed a dozen or so gold-tasseled cushions, reeking of Persia. Candlelight hid the atrocities of chipped, cheap furniture, and glowed on a table that belonged in Maxim's. Across the room, candlelight twinkled on crystal and silver and a floral centerpiece. All nice and casual.

Brad politely ignored my gawking. "Sit down and make yourself at home," he said, gesturing to the sofa. I sat, and looked at a coffee table covered with a lace cloth, on which rested a lovely crystal ashtray, a silver box holding cigarettes, and a matching silver table lighter. There were also a bottle of wine and two footed glasses.

"I've opened the wine to breathe," he mentioned.

"We wouldn't want it to suffocate."

He displayed his flashing smile in appreciation of this humor and settled on the sofa beside me to pour the wine.

"Go ahead and smoke if you want," he offered. "It dulls the palate, but when I invite company, I try to make them comfortable. I noticed you smoke, so I put out the accoutrements."

"Thank you." He kindly averted his eyes when I opened my purse to rummage amidst the welter of wallet, keys, comb, and Kleenex for my cigarettes, but as soon as I got one out, he had the lighter flaming under my nose.

This done, he turned his attention to the wine. "Pineau des Charentes," he said, lifting the bottle. "An interesting aperitif wine. This one is Château de Beaulon." He poured the ruby liquid into glasses and handed me one.

I repeated, "Thank you," and sipped, while my mind ran over clever things to say. "Very nice," I said cleverly. Nice! The word had been condemned for its dullness since the nineteenth century.

"Fruitier than the white Pineau des Charentes. I thought

you might like it before dinner. Supple, aromatic," he added, sniffing the bouquet before drinking.

"The rascal of the vineyard. It's quite sweet." I understood a dry wine was more sophisticated.

"The fermentation is muted by the brandy that's added, so it keeps its sweetness. Accidentally discovered in the fifteen hundreds in France, when a worker added brandy to the wine by mistake and hid the cask. Years later it was discovered, and this fortified wine was born. Necessity may be the mother of invention, but accident is the sire. Wonderful clarity," he informed me, holding his glass to the candle.

What I knew about wine would fit in a shot glass. I could only retaliate with words. "I guess you're an oenophile, are you not?"

"As the man said, I don't know much about wine, but I know what I like."

The ensuing monologue revealed that he did, in fact, know a great deal about wine—more than I cared to hear—but there was no stopping him. He was a veritable torrent of words. When he stopped for a breath, I derailed him.

"Will you be doing some writing while you're here, Brad?" I asked swiftly. "A treatise on modern poetry?"

"Possibly, but I'm really here to relax. I plan to do some fishing, reading, get the old body back in shape after a year at my desk," he said, thumping his lean, firm stomach. "Are you ready to eat? This dish should be served *cuit au point*—of course that applies to all cooking."

"I'm ready and waiting." My stomach emitted an audible growl to confirm it.

He drew my chair before putting dinner on a table heater. But before he put the dinner on, he had to remove the plates, which had been warming. I didn't have to turn one over to know they were Wedgwood or Minton. The aperitif wine was replaced by a Médoc, which he explained used the same grapes as the former. Nonetheless, the Médoc had to be served in fresh glasses. I bet he was wishing he'd brought along his dish washer.

"This Médoc is more subtle," he decided, after tasting it. "I like a laid-back wine with dinner."

Before he went off on another wine spiel, I said, "You've done wonders with the cottage."

"Not much so far, but I'll soon make it decent. I'm having a rug and a few things sent from my apartment. 'Gathering my creature comforts around me,' as Byron said."

"I've decided to try an ascetic work space for the summer. No distractions."

"Luxury never distracts me, but then I didn't come to work, as you did. Rosalie Hart's biography, I think you said?"

I nodded till I had swallowed a truly divine chunk of beef, tender and permeated with spices. "It's hard to believe she's still alive. She's over eighty, but still active. You wouldn't believe the stuff in her diaries and letters. She knew everyone. I'm half-afraid to use some of the material. I mean the families are still *very* influential—presidents, ambassadors, industrialists, you name it."

"They say if the past is scarlet, the book will be read. Is this American families you're talking about?"

"Some of them, but she spent a lot of time in Europe, too. Oh, crowned heads! She knew all the playboy princes."

"It sounds fascinating. Could I have a peek at the research sometime? As I said, I'm probably her number one fan." The melting glow in his eyes hinted there was room for a younger lady in his life.

"I don't see why not, if you're very careful. I'm using the original manuscripts. The ink's so faded it didn't photocopy very well. Her story will all be public knowledge soon. Of course I wouldn't want you broadcasting secrets to your colleagues. Till the book is out, we want to keep all the goodies secret."

"I'll be the soul of discretion. How did you come to get into ghostwriting, Audrey? Don't you find it restricting? The creative impulse would have to be severely stifled, I imagine."

"Not at all! Of course it's different from writing fiction. I can't change the story if I don't like it, but then in your academic writing, you're held to another person's work too, aren't you?"

"Critical analyses are interpretive work," he explained. "Fiction would be amusing, creating characters and plots to elucidate important themes, but just to tell another person's story . . . You must have a very small ego, Audrey."

My hackles began to lift. "Not as large as some. I've never cultivated a bloated ego."

"Ego is just another word for self. If there's a lot of self to be accommodated . . ." He hunched his shoulders.

This oblique comment on the insignificant stature of my ego cut me to the quick. I would *not* argue with him! I was having a superb dinner with a handsome, intelligent man, and I would gush if it killed me. "This is a wonderful dish," I gushed, and dipped a crusty French bread into the last of the sauce.

It worked. He stopped bragging and smiled. "I enjoy puttering around the kitchen. I don't know why women despise it. I'm afraid dessert is only fresh strawberries and clotted cream, but I can vouch for the coffee. I have it specially blended."

Every berry was a ruby jewel. There wasn't a white-centered, sour one in the lot. The coffee was perfect too, deep and mellow with no bitter aftertaste. We took it to the sofa and relaxed against the velvet cushions. I felt like the queen of the harem, but a tiny suspicion was sprouting that my companion was no sultan. When a man is so actively interested in interior decorating and cooking, there's a tendency to check the firmness of his wrists.

"Now I'll allow myself the luxury of a cigarette," he decided, and helped himself from the silver box on the table. "A little Cointreau with your coffee?" The wrist lifting the Cointreau looked firm enough.

"I'm sated."

"Oh, sorry!"

"No, I meant it as a compliment!"

"You mean you're replete. I was afraid I'd stuffed you past comfort."

What I take to less kindly than anything else is having my grammar and/or vocabulary corrected, especially when I'm wrong. "Actually I meant sated, but it's not your fault I stuffed myself. I feel like a Strasbourg goose."

He smiled forgivingly. "I should have known a writer would say what she meant. I'll skip the Cointreau and have it later for a sleeping draft. When can I have a look at Rosalie's diaries?"

"Any time you want. I can get some now if . . ."

He held me down by putting a hand on my arm, and melted me with an intimate smile. "I'm not in that big a rush. I'd prefer to get better acquainted with you tonight, and meet Rosalie tomorrow."

I ransacked my brain for something interesting to say, but I'd shot my bolt in bragging about Rosalie's biography.

"Where are you from?" he prodded.

The smoke from our cigarettes mingled in the air above us. Candlelight, the exotic surroundings, and especially the model-perfect man beside me created an aura of romantic unreality, as ephemeral as the smoke above. The last thing I wanted to do was drag in reality. In less than two minutes I sketched the history of my life. Born and raised in Brooklyn; university; and the remove to the East Side of New York, where I'd got a precarious foot in the door of publishing. It didn't take much of an ego to hold my story, or my "self."

Brad made a more interesting tale of his boyhood exploits in Ireland, his graduation from Dublin University (with a double first), to the English publication of his first critical work, which got picked up in the States, where it caused some stir in literary circles. This led to an offer of a teaching post, so he'd picked up and come to the States.

"I have a copy of my book here. Since you're interested in modern poetry, you might want to look through it," he said, and went to a bookcase.

He handed me a slim volume bound in morocco leather with gold trim. *The Art of Eliot*, it was called. A quick flip through showed me such intimidating and pretentious words as *prelapsarian*, *specious good*, and *coercive evil*. "It looks fascinating. Thanks," I said, and slid it in my bag.

"I haven't scratched the surface of *The Waste Land*," he admitted. "This was my first attempt at literary criticism. I've gained more mature insights since then. Maybe I'll start to analyze them this summer, while you type Rosalie's biography."

He would engage in his deep, cerebral, serious work, while *I* typed. The man was insufferable! "Actually I have to write it, before it can be typed up. Since you're so fastidious about words, I just mention it." The voice in which I mentioned it was waspish, but he didn't take offense. He was too busy preparing more insults.

"A slip of the tongue. I'd be happy to look over your

work before you submit it, if you like," he offered. "If it's well written, the book clubs might take it up. There should be a serious theme in Rosalie's life. The legendry of the American dream—the sort of thing Fitzgerald handled so well in fiction, and so abominably in practice."

I counted to ten, and should have gone on counting till I simmered down, but the silence was stretching noticeably. "The rags-to-riches-to-ruin theme is pretty well worn by now. I wouldn't dream of wasting your valuable time. The public won't be looking for philsophy when they buy this book. They already know the story; they want the intimate details."

"Of course, a sort of long gossip column." He nodded patronizingly. "You don't want a literary critic getting his heavy hands on a work of light entertainment. It was just an idea."

I opened my mouth to remind him that critics were lice on the locks of literature, when he spoke up to subdue my hackles. "To be honest, it was an excuse to see more of you."

A frank, warm smile creased his beautiful wrinkles. My resentment vanished like dew in the noonday sun, leaving hardly a trace. Here I thought I'd been making a terrible impression on him. That he'd made a terrible one on me was beside the point. "I'll be pretty busy, but I'm sure we can work something out."

"I know how hard you'll be working, that's why I was trying to find an excuse to hang around. It was a dumb, arrogant thing for me to say to an established writer like you. Blame it on my profession. Once a teacher, you know . . . But you won't be working day and night, I hope?"

"I only work during the day."

"That leaves us the best time—the nights." The warmth

had suddenly escalated to sultry, suggestive heat. His eyes looked ready to let off steam. "It was incredible luck, finding such a beautiful, intelligent neighbor. The luck of the Irish, downright serendipitous," he said softly, and squeezed my fingers.

"Same here." I agreed enthusiastically. "I thought I'd be stuck with old Simcoe for company. He barges in about ten times a day to see if I've broken any of his cracked dishes, or marked his Woolworth antiques. He's quite a character." A look of surprise, or impatience, on Brad's face made me realize I had just botched a romantic opening.

"Yeah, I—you should put him in one of your books." He laughed and clapped his forehead with the heel of his palm. "Stupid of me. You don't do fiction, of course. See how you've rattled my poor old brains?"

"We'll blame it on the Château de—whatever. It's made me a bit sleepy."

He peered at his Rolex. "It's not late."

"I'm planning to do a little research before I go to bed."

"But the nights were supposed to be reserved for us!"

"I'm sure you have things to do—settle into your new digs."

"I still have some unpacking to do, and I've got a good book to keep me company too. *The Logic of Scientific Discovery*, by Karl Popper. Terrific book. Have you read it?"

I'd never even heard of it. "I don't read much in the scientific line."

He blinked in confusion. "It's philosophy."

"Oh, *that* Popper."

"I'll lend it to you when I've finished. Don't pay any attention to my margin jottings. You'll love the book."

While he went to his desk to get it, I strolled to the bookcase. The weighty tomes resting there aroused all my old feelings of inferiority. Philosophy, essays, poetry, with a sprinkling of modern paperbacks. Looking more closely, I noticed a dozen or so by Madison Gantry, a popular writer of men's racy detective fiction.

Brad suddenly hovered at my shoulder. "Escape reading," he explained. "There's a little more to them than the sitcoms on TV at least. Gantry isn't quite as illiterate as most of the escape writers. Have you ever read him at all?"

"No, my brand of escape is romance. I like Rosalie Wildewood a lot."

"Try this one—I think you'll like it." He handed me a Gantry.

I stuffed it in my purse with the book on Eliot. "I'll leave you to Popper. See you tomorrow."

"I'll walk you home," he offered.

It hardly seemed necessary, but I'd left the lights off and the door unlocked, so I was glad for the company. "I'll go in and wait till you have a look around," he said.

"I don't suppose they have many muggers here in the country."

"They have raccoons, skunks, and other undesirable critters."

He came in and waited while I turned on the lights and looked around. He strolled to the table and took a diary from my box of research material. "Mind if I take this home with me? I'll bring it back tomorrow."

I looked to see it wasn't a book I needed right away, and told him to take it. "But don't lose it. I have to give all this stuff back to Rosalie."

"I'll be careful." At the doorway, he stopped and turned around. "Thanks again," he said, looking at the diary.

"Thank you for the feast."

After a thirty-second silent pause, during which he looked a question at me, and I apparently gave approval, he drew me into his arms. Even in heels, I had the luxury of reaching up to put my arms lightly around him. His head came down and stopped two inches above mine. "Did I happen to tell you, you're sensational?" he asked softly.

"It must have slipped your mind," I murmured.

"Not for one minute," he said, and kissed me.

I hadn't realized he was so strong till I felt his arms crushing the breath from my lungs, shaping my body to his. Warm fingers moved over my back, their heat passing through my light silk blouse. Brad kissed the way he cooked—*au point*. Just the right amount of enthusiasm and pressure to show it was more than a formality, without overwhelming me. The ingredients were right, too; a woodsy scent hovered discreetly around him at this close range. His lips firmed, and a palpable excitement spiced with a soupçon of passion swelled between us. It was a natural chemistry, which took its course, simmering long enough to leave me breathless. I knew in my melting bones that I could easily lose my head over this man.

His index finger stroked my cheek in a delightfully possessive and familiar way. He said, "See you tomorrow. Sleep tight."

I drifted into the living room on a cloud. I had just spent the evening with a tall, literate, heterosexual male older than twenty and younger than sixty. A man who didn't consider kissing one of the martial arts. How had I gotten so lucky? He was interesting, handsome, even rich. And he liked me. He thought I was intelligent and beautiful. He thought I was sensational. Nobody ever called me "sensational" before in my whole life. When I stopped in front of the mirror over the sofa, I looked almost beautiful. There was a dreamy smile on my lips, and stars in my eyes.

It would be intellectually stimulating to see him. Philosophy and real literature—I used to be interested in those things when I was at college. I foresaw a wonderful summer of rewarding work and pleasant diversion, culminating in—Now be real. Keep one moccasin on the ground. Culminating in the completed biography of Rosalie, and some more money.

I glanced through a few of Rosalie's letters, but my heart wasn't in it, so I took Brad's book of critical essays on Eliot to bed with me. It was wonderfully erudite, and the only reason my eyes were closing was that I was tired. If I remembered *The Waste Land* better, I'd understand the essays, find them more interesting. But what the hell was the "specious good," and what did "prelapsarian" mean anyway? It wasn't even in my dictionary. It meant he was a deep-dyed intellectual, and would soon discover I was shallow and superficial, with no real self to fill up my ego. But he hadn't found it out yet, and Helen was in Greece on her honeymoon, so there'd be no interference from that quarter.

How had she gotten Garth to the altar so fast? To me, he used to talk about "a few years from now," after he was settled more securely in his career. In a few years, I'd be thirty. I was *ancient*. I felt Time clawing at my back. Helen was thirty, and made no bones about wanting to get married. If Helen were here, Brad would be on his knees proposing before the end of the summer. How did she do it? What was the trick?

It seemed almost impossible that Brad had turned up here, in the woods of northern New York. What was a man like that doing here? Even I found the cottages awful, and he was used to the best. For privacy, he could have gone anywhere—to Cape Cod, or some quiet corner of Mexico, or Majorca. There had to be a lead lining in this bright and breezy cloud.

CHAPTER 3

Just as I was settling in at my desk the next morning, I heard Brad's screen door bang. I hurried to the window for a glimpse of him. There he was, running along past the window in a navy fleecy and white shorts, which gave a stunning view of his long, tanned legs. In his white Reeboks and with a red sweatband around his head, he looked as if he'd just jogged out of a high school gym. He lifted an arm in friendly salute; I waved back, already feeling proprietarial.

The presence of a critic next door should have been enough to distract me, but it didn't. I considered it a goad, and a challenge. The words *specious good* and *prelapsarian* didn't actually appear on my pages, but I began to perceive some deeper meaning than mere entertainment in Rosalie's story. I missed seeing Brad jog home, but that afternoon I spotted him down at Simcoe's dock, getting into a boat with a fishing rod over his shoulder

While he was out fishing, a small moving van stopped at his cottage, and as he wasn't there, the driver came to mine.

"You can just leave the things in his cottage," I suggested.

"We can't get in, lady. The door's locked, and some-body's got to sign."

"Locked? That's funny. I guess you'd better put the things in my cottage then."

They deposited an oriental carpet, a vacuum cleaner, boxes labeled FRAGILE, and a modern chair, all chrome and leather, of the sort immortalized by Mies van der Rohe. The old traditional and the best of the modern—it seemed symbolic of Brad. I tried the chair and found it uncomfortable. When I saw Brad wending his way up from the dock with his rod, I called out to tell him I had his things.

"You locked your door. Are you afraid of the wild critters, or me?"

"Force of habit, I guess. I'll be right over. I have to put this gear away. Got any cold beer?"

"Coming right up." I hurried in to brush my hair and put on some lipstick. It was five o'clock, and time to take my hard-earned leisure. The book was going great, which always put me in a good mood.

He was soon at the door, lounging in with only a preliminary tap. A day in the sun had deepened his tan to a rich, warm bronze. The white shirt contrasted sharply with it.

"How was the fishing? Did you catch anything?"

"Not yet. I was testing the water, and my lures. I see my Barcelona chair arrived. I can't get comfortable on that lumpy sofa."

"Sit yourself down on it, and I'll get the beer. What have you done with yourself all day?" I asked, to conceal that I'd monitored his every movement.

"I jogged my four miles this morning, did a bit of housecleaning before that. I spotted some wild mushrooms when I was out jogging. It was a temptation, but they can be dangerous. Incidentally, I hope you like chicken Marengo.

It's not too late to change the menu if you don't," he said, with a questioning look.

"If it was good enough for Napoleon, it's good enough for me. Does this mean I'm invited for dinner again?"

"I hope you'll come. Presumptuous of me . . ."

"Presume away—I'm free. I'll have to cook you a meal one of these days," I said rashly.

"You're too busy. And I like cooking. I finished Rosalie's diary over lunch. A certain supreme court judge won't be too happy to hear his father dallied with Rosalie, but it should be good for sales."

"Shocking, huh? There's another you should take a look at—the father of one of our past presidents, and the worst skinflint in the world. He gave her jewelry, and took it back when she broke off with him."

"It just goes to show you," he said, and took a drink from the bottle. He had glanced at Rosalie's painting a few times. Its brilliant colors stood out like a new cushion on an old sofa in the dingy room. "That's an interesting painting. Not quite in harmony with Simcoe's rubbish. It must be your own. It's Rosalie, isn't it?"

"Yes, a self-portrait. She gave it to me."

"Really?" He struggled out of the Barcelona chair and walked toward it. "It's very good. It could pass for a Pissarro, or do I mean Seurat? One of the pointillists anyway. I wouldn't have thought Rosalie would have the patience to do it, all those little dots of color, like confetti."

"The man who framed it for me called it the 'Polka Dot Nude.' I think it's lovely."

He backed away to allow the dots to merge into a pattern, and I regaled him with its history, as told by Rosalie. "Rosalie was kind of an art groupie. She hung out with that set in France on her holidays. Early in her career she started painting, and when she retired from work, it became an avocation. She did this picture in the south of France, at Picasso's studio. Jean Cocteau was there, Le´ger, and Villon. She and Cocteau spent an evening doing it with confetti from an old photograph, then Picasso opened a door and the whole thing blew away, so she decided to paint it. She could have been a good artist, if she'd exerted herself in that direction."

"She *is* pretty good, to judge by this. Did you see any other of her works?"

"She was working on an abstract expressionist thing when I was at Hartland. Of course her eyesight isn't what it was, but I didn't care for it. I know painting's been her hobby for ages, but she didn't have any others on display. Some of them must be worth a lot of money. She mentioned that Picasso had drawn a girl, and she painted it. She might have had help from other famous artists as well—she knew them all. I certainly treasure this."

"Paintings by famous people have some interest value, even if they're not top quality. A Churchill, for instance, would be something to treasure," Brad said. "I wonder what she did with them."

"She probably gave them away, as she gave me this one. Or maybe her daughter has them."

Brad's head jerked up. "Daughter?" he asked, in a loud voice.

"She doesn't admit she has one, but there's a year or so of her life that isn't very well accounted for. Her diaries from that period are sketchy, to say the least. She misplaced one, she said. The last one before that mentions gaining ten pounds, and in a letter she received from a friend there's a question about whether she's feeling better. After the war, Rosalie had what she calls a nervous breakdown, and went to a clinic in Europe to dry out."

"Oh, really? Whereabouts in Europe?"

"She says it was a spa in Switzerland, but I haven't been able to corroborate it in her diaries. They're not complete, by any means. There are a few suspicious entries—mentions of stomach upset and weight gain, then there's blank till she returns home. I tried to question her companion, but came up against a brick wall."

"Who is her companion?"

"A woman named Lorraine Taylor—she used to be Rosalie's stand-in. She always went with Rosalie everywhere, and when they came back to the States, Lorraine had a new daughter with her. The girl's name is Drew Taylor. Lorraine was officially married, although she hadn't lived with her husband for years. He was a prop man in Hollywood. Rosalie was single at the time."

"And you think Rosalie was the real mother, that they fudged the records somehow?"

"I think so. In those days, an illegitimate child wasn't considered good publicity. The Hays Office influence. Rosalie was trying to make a comeback, but it didn't take. Before long, she married an oil tycoon and gave up films for good. And even when she was married, Lorraine and Drew still lived with Rosalie. It kind of makes you wonder."

"Who do you figure the father was, if she really had this child?" Brad asked. He was frowning, maybe disillusioned with his heroine.

"She had a hot and heavy affair with a French director before she left for Europe, but according to Drew Taylor's birth date, he can't be the one. It would have to be somebody she met while abroad. I haven't given up getting the whole story out of her."

His frown deepened. "People are entitled to some privacy, even aging actresses who have to sell their stories to survive."

"She's not exactly starving. She could sell Hartland for a

couple of million. She's just bored, being out of the limelight."

Brad finished his beer, and I offered to help him take his belongings to his cottage. I smiled to see a microwave oven unpacked, along with one of those impossible machines that slices, dices, minces, mashes, shreds, and otherwise makes food unrecognizable. I always wondered who'd be fool enough to buy one.

"Now, Audrey, I suggest you take advantage of what's left of the sun, while I start dinner," Brad said.

"Yes, boss. I'll let myself out." I didn't want to delay his cooking.

On my way through the living room, I noticed one of the Madison Gantry books was open, facedown, on the coffee table. Between Rosalie's diary, which he had finished reading, and this book, entitled *Serenade for a Sinner*, I didn't think he'd had much time for Popper's philosophy. I took an hour of late-afternoon sun on the dock before dressing for dinner. The sun wasn't hot enough to tint my Pillsbury Doughboy body, but it felt good.

It was another wonderful evening. Aware now that his casual was my semiformal, I wore a green and white skirt and scrounged through drawers till I found a blouse to go with it. It was only a simple peasant blouse, off the shoulders, but with some lace trim to enliven it. The music at Brad's cottage was recognizable on that occasion: Chopin, played by Rubinstein. It was the food I didn't recognize. He had gone to the bother of making hors d'oeuvres, which sat in state on the coffee table on the hot tray.

The setting sun slanted through immaculate windows— when had he had time to clean them?—casting a golden glow on the oriental carpet, already installed underfoot.

"I have breaded oysters and eggplant fingers to go with

our aperitif wine," he explained, as he handed me a plate and serviette. "I'm serving the white Pineau des Charentes with this. Coq d'Or, it's called. Let me know what you think."

Brad was looking rather appetizing himself, with a sports shirt open at the neck beneath his jacket, giving him a more casual air. As the aroma from the hors d'oeuvres wafted toward him, however, I turned my attention to them. They were so good it was impossible to stop eating till they were gone.

"You should be a chef," I told him. "Open your own restaurant—you'd make a killing."

"Actually I *do* have an interest in a little place in New York. Le Pavillon d'Antibes, it's called. You may have heard of it?"

"No, but I'll certainly look it up when I get back. Who runs it for you?"

"My chef's name is Pierre Leblanc, from Paris. We work out the recipes and menus together. Pierre swears by Escoffier, but I'm working on him to be more venturesome."

"How can a professor afford to buy a restaurant?"

"I have my writing as well."

"You know, Brad, I can't figure out what brought a man like you to this backwater for the summer. Why didn't you go to Spain, or something? You obviously don't like roughing it in the bush, or you wouldn't have brought so many things with you."

"Just a change of pace—I like the fishing and fresh air. And the company." He smiled, in a way that made me forget further questions.

If the chicken Marengo hadn't been so irresistible, I couldn't have done it justice. His apologies for not having concocted a dessert were heard with relief.

Somehow, a box of Godiva chocolates had found its way to the coffee table, and had to be sampled. They were so pretty it seemed a shame to eat them. "I'm going to put on about fifty pounds if I keep doing this," I lamented happily as he poured the coffee. Brad turned on the radio to avoid having to select records.

He ran his dark eyes over my anatomy. "All the more of you to admire," he smiled. "Women worry too much about their weight. You certainly don't have to."

"It's not just the weight, it's the distribution."

"The distribution curves look pretty good to me. Would you like to go out somewhere?" he asked suddenly. "I'm showing you a flat time, expecting my unadorned company to keep you entertained."

"There isn't much to do around here. That's why I chose the place, to keep my nose to the grindstone."

He ran a playful finger along my nose. "Why would you want to wear that pretty little nose to a point?"

Tall, lanky women don't have much chance to feel cute. I realized what we were missing. I felt cute and cuddly and cherished when he put his arm around me and pressed my head against his shoulder.

"On the other hand," he went on in a relaxed drawl, "I don't know why we should go out, when we're so comfortable here. Good wine, good company—what more could we want?"

I sighed contentedly and said, "Search me."

Brad's head angled down. "That's the best offer I've had all day," he said, softening it with a smile. "Where do you suggest I begin?"

His eyes strayed to the top of my blouse, which had a tendency to gap when I was sitting down. Before his hand decided to follow his eyes, I took it and put it at my waist.

"What you sees is what you—" An incipient smile alerted me to danger. "Is all there is."

"And I don't get it, right?" He laughed. "All that pulchritude—seems a waste."

"You must subscribe to the theory that good things come in small packages. I'm scrawny."

"Willowy."

"We'll compromise. I'm thin."

" 'Less is more'—Browning."

"Also the motto of modern architects. The same guys who tell us houses are machines for living in, and by corollary I suppose women are for—"

"You're putting words in my mouth!"

"Fine, just so I don't put ideas in your head."

Meanwhile our hands were involved in a power struggle, mine trying to hold his down. When he realized I wasn't kidding, he pulled away, and looked sheepish. "Sorry, I guess I got carried away."

"Feet first, next time," I warned, but lightly, to show I wasn't really shocked or horrified.

He moved along to the far end of the sofa and examined me for a minute, then said, rather tentatively, "A lot of people nowadays are into celibacy?" His inflection made it a question, and his eyes revealed why he wanted to know.

For a fleeting moment, I caught a resemblance to Garth in him. The indirect question, the interest that didn't want to quite reveal itself, in case of rejection. "I've been reading that too. Personally, I just like to know a man well before I know him intimately." I was pleased with this well-balanced assertion, and cast a cool, bright smile on him.

His answering smile was less cool. He nodded, as though accepting it, and said, "Fine, we'll talk and become well acqainted." But already he'd left his corner and was shimmying along the sofa toward me. "I appreciate that restraint in a woman," he said. His voice sounded as though he were eating marshmallows. Within two seconds, his arm reached for my waist.

"I'd appreciate a little of it from you as well." I flicked his fingers away as though they were flies. "Funny, you know, I didn't take you for a sex fiend. You seemed so civilized when I first met you."

The offending hand was slowly withdrawn. His eyes narrowed momentarily, then he settled back and let a grin steal across his lips. "'Fiend' is overdoing it, surely. I'm passionate. You know what they say. If you don't play, you can't win. Are you afraid to play the game of life?"

I gave him a derisive smile. "Children play games, Brad. I'm not a child, and I'm not susceptible to fuzzy amateur psychology."

His good humor remained unimpaired. "Not to that particular line," he countered.

"I'm sure you have a dozen others you're dying to cast out. Testing your lures, as unsuccessfully as you did this afternoon. I had hoped to have some interesting conversation with an intellectual like you."

He was ridiculously susceptible to this line. We talked about novels and our writing. I admitted to a forlorn hope of someday writing a serious novel; he admitted there was a lack of satisfaction in literary criticism, and a lack of financial reward too, which made me wonder how he'd bought half a French restaurant. The radio played softly in the background, hardly noticed. If it hadn't been for the startling words "Rosalie Hart," we wouldn't have heard it at all. We both jumped and looked at each other with shocked eyes, while the announcer contained.

"Rosalie Hart, former star of stage and screen, died today in her home, Hartland, in California. The doctor has announced she choked on caviar, while sharing a bottle of champagne with her companion, Lorraine Taylor. The death was accidental. Foul play is not suspected. Details of the funeral will be announced later."

"My God, she's dead!" I gasped.

Brad's reaction was possibly stronger than my own. He turned a shade paler, before he jumped up and ran to the radio, to turn up the volume, but the announcer had already gone on to the next item.

"What a shock for you!" he exclaimed.

"I can't believe it."

"It's the end of an era." He sat down and stared at the floor.

"I wonder how this will affect my book. Brad, I'm going home and turning on the TV. There might be something, some more details."

"I'll go with you, if you don't mind. I'd like to hear it too, and I don't have a TV."

We went to my place, but the regular TV programs were in progress. "Maybe the late news will have something," I said. "I'm going to call my editor. She might not have heard."

"I'll run along then, but do you mind if I come back for the late news?"

"Of course not."

I had to go over to Simcoe's to make the call, since my phone wasn't being installed till the next morning. I was grudgingly admitted, and after a little haggling, it was agreed I'd ask for the long-distance charge and pay him on the spot. After all that, my editor wasn't home. I'd have to call her first thing in the morning.

"How are you and young O'Malley making out?" Mr. Simcoe asked. His wife was not visible, though I heard a rocking chair creaking in the next room. It stopped to allow her better hearing of my answer.

"Just fine. Brad's very nice."

"It's too bad you've got to work so hard. It hardly seems worth his while coming, when you're so busy all day."

"I don't think I'm the only reason he's here, Mr. Simcoe." I laughed.

He looked quite surprised at this. What strange world did he inhabit, that he thought a man like Brad O'Malley would come seeking out somebody like me, in the wilderness?

"He mentioned the fishing," he said doubtfully.

"Yes. Well, thanks for the use of the phone. There won't be any charge after all. I couldn't reach my editor."

"You won't have to pay for using it then." His suspenders expanded with this beneficence, and he accompanied me to the door.

I went back to my cottage and watched TV. Rosalie's death didn't bother me in a deeply emotional way. I hadn't known her well enough or long enough for that. To me, the major concern was how it would affect my book. I turned the volume down and left the picture on, glancing at the screen once in a while, while I looked over my research.

At ten, Brad came back, bringing the borrowed diary with him. "It's too bad she didn't live another six months, and then this death would have been a big boost for my book," I said.

"That's a pretty crude way to look at it," he said, rather sharply.

"Take it easy! I was just thinking out loud. So it was selfish, but if she was going to die anyway, it would have been good for me if she'd died when the book was ready for release. Do you want some coffee?" I asked, to smooth his ruffled feathers.

"No, thanks," He just sat staring at the screen, as though his mind were miles away, till the item came on. Rosalie had been big enough in her day that her death led off the news. They had accumulated a short tape on her life, showing cuts from a few of her hit movies, and some personal footage as well. Most of it had been seen before; all of it was at least twenty-five years old.

"Well, that's the end of Rosalie Hart," Brad said sadly. "I wish I'd known her."

"You sound as though you're half in love with her."

"Maybe—half. At my age, death's upsetting."

"Your age!" I laughed. "How old are you anyway? All of thirty-four or -five, I imagine."

He gave a self-conscious look that made me raise his probable age a few years. "Thereabouts. I won't sleep much tonight. Is it all right if I take another of her diaries?"

"Help yourself. I wish I had something really boring to put me to sleep."

Then I remembered *The Art of Eliot*, and knew my problem was solved. Brad took a while, sorting through the volumes.

"Are you looking for anything in particular?"

"What you were talking about—the period when she was in Europe, and you think she had a baby."

"I told you, that space of time is missing, Brad. Try this one," I said, and offered him one of the racier books.

"You mentioned one where she complained of gaining weight." He kept rooting till he found the one he wanted.

He left, with no romantic interlude that night. He seemed awfully preoccupied, and I couldn't believe it was the thought of his own death that caused it. It was Rosalie's. Funny how attached people became to movie stars. You'd almost think he had known her personally. She wasn't a coeval of his. I remembered how upset people had been when Elvis Presley died, and John Lennon was killed. But that was different—it was people the same age as the stars who had felt that deeply about the deaths. Rosalie was old enough to be Brad's grandmother. Of course what he was mourning wasn't the wrinkled little woman I knew, but the winsome face seen on the screen. The face smiling at me from the gilt frame.

I went to bed, and was soon lulled to sleep by *The Art of Eliot*, and the gentle lap of water against the rocky shore.

CHAPTER 4

As soon as Bell installed my phone the next morning, I called Eileen Haddon. My editor had already heard about Rosalie's death.

"Bad news for us, huh?" I asked.

"That's debatable. If we could get your book out soon, it would help sales. What's your best date on the manuscript?"

"My deadline's October. I'll be ready by then, not much sooner."

A nervous laugh trickled down the wire. "I hope you can do better than that. Is August out of the question? August the first, I mean?"

"August! Eileen, look at your calendar. It's late June already."

"Is it absolutely out of the question?" she persisted.

"Absolutely."

"Well, do it as quickly as you can. The end of August is already later than we want. There's a TV special planned, and some talk of a Rosalie Hart movie festival as well. The magazines will do something, and we'd like to cash in on the free publicity. Belton is going to put out one of their trashy quickies, an unauthorized biography. In fact, Mason is at work on it already. Hume Mason, the king of quickies, began one last month, as soon as Belton heard we were doing Rosalie."

My insides clenched up like a fist at this news. Panic warred with pride. I guess it was pride that said, "I wanted to make this really good, a meaningful book."

"Of course, Audrey, but do it fast too." Eileen was obviously ruled by panic. "Send me in what you've got. I'll edit as you go along, to save time. How many chapters are done?"

"Two, but they're only in rough. They have to be polished and retyped."

"Two chapters?" she howled. "What have you been doing all this time?"

"I've got about fifty pounds of research to digest."

"I know. Guard it with your life. The estate will want it back in good order. Keep yourself informed on the funeral too. It might make a good closing chapter. Wraps it all up nice and tidy. I'll let you get back to work now. Work hard! Bye."

I muttered to myself as I banged down the receiver. "Work hard. What do you think I've been doing, playing the violin?"

I went at it harder than before, only stopping at noon to grab an apple and a slice of rye bread. I could do with some reducing after Brad's gluttonous feasts. I wondered if he'd make me dinner again, after I'd refused to go along with his fun and games last night. I hadn't lowered myself to buying meals and company at the price of my body, if that was all he was after. I wasn't ready for another devastating jilting either, and that was the likeliest conclusion to an affair with Brad. First I had to staunch the bleeding from losing Garth.

By four, the ache between my shoulders told me I'd

overdone it. My head throbbed, and my sentences were all turning compound. It came as a surprise when I looked out the window and remembered where I was. Tall pines hewn to grotesque shapes by the wind replaced the more familiar skyscrapers. Instead of solid concrete, sun-dappled grass waved underfoot. Through the rear window the river was visible, rippled by wind and sparkling. Brad's car was home. I changed into shorts and a halter and went to the rocky shore to test the water with my toes. It was perishingly cold. The dock between my cottage and Brad's was a good place for sunbathing. A derelict striped canvas chair coaxed me into its sagging nest. It felt exactly like the famous Barcelona chair—very uncomfortable. Simcoe's boat was at his dock, so Brad wasn't out fishing. Maybe he'd started another essay on poetry.

After angling the chair to gather the maximum rays from the sun, I half closed my eyes and gazed dreamily across the water. That was Canada over there, so close you could swim to it, if the currents allowed. The St. Lawrence was a mile wide here, Simcoe had told me. Two enormous ships crossed in the seaway, with a haunting hoot from their horns. It was a sound often heard at night in bed, eerie and unsettling, like a distant train whistle, carrying a hint of excitement and far-off places. All so peaceful and different from New York. A nice place to visit, but how could anyone bear to live there? Didn't the constant racket of the crickets drive them around the bend?

Brad must be tired of working by now. I'd go and ask him if he wanted a beer. In fact, I wanted one myself. I went to my cottage, planning to take two over to his place, to sniff the air for dinner. When I opened the door, I got the fright of my life. There was a man there, at my desk, his head bent over my box of research, which he was riffling through. The soft pad of my bare feet hid my approach from him. With my eyes dazzled from the sun, I didn't recognize Brad for a minute.

My voice was rough with shock. "What are you doing?" I demanded.

His head came up then, and I realized who it was. "I just came to ask you if I could borrow another of those interesting books for tonight. Sorry if I frightened you. Is it okay if I take this?"

"I guess so, but please don't take anything without asking me. Remember, these are the originals, and there aren't any copies. I was just coming to get a beer. Would you like one?"

"Sure, why don't we take it down to the dock and have a swim first? The water's quite clean here."

"It's also frigid. Just ask my toe—the blue one. It's been in."

"You're not afraid of a little cold water, are you?" He laughed. "A big girl like you."

"Big girl" ranks second only to correcting my grammar in insults. I'm not a big girl, I'm a tall woman. "Maybe it's not too cold for a big boy like you," I said, and got the beer.

He didn't seem to mind being insulted. "Come down to the dock and keep me company anyway. I've got to go home and change first."

I took four beers in a pail with ice down to the dock, and was comfortably sagging in the deck chair when Brad arrived. I thought he'd look like this in bathing trunks: a golden, muscled, tapering torso; the chest not overly hirsute, but with a good masculine path of hair. Great legs, long and straight. I also suspected he'd wear white to optimize his tan. If I half closed my eyes, I could imagine it was last summer, and I was looking at Garth. I opened my eyes, and noticed Brad was making a close scrutiny of my own white body. At least he wasn't scowling. Far from it.

To lighten the mood, I tucked my tongue under my bottom lip and let out a wolf whistle. "You must pump iron," I complimented.

"No way, it deforms the pecs and glutes. I jog, play raquetball, ski, swim. Actually swimming is the perfect exercise," he said over his shoulder as he took a pose at the end of the wooden dock, trapezoids rippling. For the next twenty minutes, all I saw of him was his head turning to the side to breathe, and his arms knifing smoothly through the water. He swam to a distant island, then turned around and swam back, without resting. Pretty good for a man his age. Was that why he worked out so hard, to retain his boyish figure? Vain creature.

He wasn't breathing so very hard when he climbed out. "Show off," I said, in a desultory, unimpressed voice, and opened another bottle of beer. "Here, you've earned this."

He stretched out on the dock. "How's the work going?" he asked. "I haven't seen you out all day." When he lay down, the heaving of his chest was more noticeable. He sounded quite winded too.

"I'm in high gear, and may have to go into overdrive. I have competition. Belton—the big paperback people—are putting out a hack job on Rosalie. A guy named Hume Mason specializes in this sort of thing."

"I've heard of him. He's done quite a few, hasn't he?"

"About half a dozen, I guess."

"I liked his one on Dean Mathers, the rock star who O.D.'d a couple of years ago. He caught the flashy, sleazy life-style very well," Brad said, and turned his face to the sun.

"Flash and sleaze—he'd be good at that. He's kind of a specialist in it."

"That's unprofessional, Audrey, cutting up the competition. What's the matter, jealous?" he teased.

"Jealous of that creep! You've got to be kidding. He's just exploiting Rosalie, making a quick buck on her death."

When he turned his head and looked at me, his smile wore a jeering edge. "I seem to remember you regretted she couldn't have timed her death more conveniently."

"That's different. I'm doing an authorized biography. I got the facts from the horse's mouth, not gossip from old scandal sheets."

"You got the facts she was willing to dole out. Mason's book will be less biased."

The fact that he had closed his eyes again annoyed me. If you're going to have an argument, the least your enemy can do is look at you. "I'm surprised a high-brow professor like you has ever read anything by Mason," I retorted. "But then I guess you have pretty catholic tastes. Eliot and Gantry—from the sublime to the ridiculous."

"Oh, I wouldn't say Eliot's ridiculous," he said, in a drawling voice.

"He's a pendantic bore, and you know perfectly well I meant Gantry is ridiculous."

"You tried his book, did you?"

"No."

"But you could tell by the naked woman on the cover it wasn't any good. I think you should have a swim, Audrey. We'll blame your lousy mood on overwork."

I was in a lousy mood all right, and in a way it was overwork that caused it, but the only reason I was overworked was Hume Mason. I let the air clear for a few minutes before saying anything. "I wonder when Rosalie's funeral will be. I hope it's on TV. I want to see how she's dispatched. It'll likely be a huge, Hollywood-style funeral."

"It's the day after tomorrow. I didn't hear what kind of a do's in progress. I heard it on my car radio when I went into town to buy a fishing rod today. I stopped for a hamburger on the way home, since I'm going fishing tonight. Want to come?"

I had skimped on lunch in anticipation of another feast. If there's anything more boring than drowning worms, I don't know what it can be. "I don't think so. I have a bunch of letters I'm matching up with one of Rosalie's diaries, trying to get a few facts straightened out. I'll pass."

We finished our beer with no further bickering. While I scrambled two eggs and burned some toast, I saw Brad go over to Simcoe's dock with his fishing rod. As twilight fell, the cottage seemed dull and dark and lonely, so I went out to watch the sun set on the river. Before I'd been there two minutes, Mr. Simcoe came pattering over for a chat.

"Not fishing, eh?" he asked, snapping his suspenders.

"No, I don't care for it."

"Don't worry. He won't stay out long."

"I'm not worried," I said, swift to imagine a slur on my magnetic powers.

"You ought to give him a good talking-to. You have to work all day and he goes out fishing at night. That's no way for a fellow to behave with his girl friend."

I laughed at his romanticism. But Brad and I were probably his major entertainment for the summer, and to fashion a love affair between us would amuse him endlessly. It seemed a shame to disillusion him. "We're just friends," I said.

He laughed merrily. "You don't fool me. I've had a few chats with Mr. O'Malley."

"What did he say?" I asked, startled.

"Nothing but compliments."

What innocent remark had Simcoe revised into a grand passion? I wondered if he planned to hang around and pester me till I went inside. His wife soon came to the door and called him. "Phone, Eddie," she said, but their windows were wide open, and the phone hadn't rung. I think the woman was actually jealous. I soon went inside, and passed the evening reading my research and watching TV for any new items on Rosalie. I also kept an eye out the window for Brad's return. I didn't see him come back, but around nine, I noticed there was a light on in his cottage. The curtains were closely drawn, but little strips of light seeped through around the edges. He'd probably just left the lights on when he left. It stayed bright so late I hadn't noticed it before. Simcoe's boat wasn't back, but unless Brad O'Malley was already in that cottage at nine, he didn't get back till after twelve. That was when I finally dozed off to sleep. Did men fish from six till twelve? Lord, how boring.

The combination of the early sunrise and the flimsy curtains usually got me up around seven-thirty in the morning. I was just coming out of the shower when someone knocked at the front door. I pulled my terry dressing gown tightly around me, bundled my wet hair up in a towel turban, and opened the door a crack. Nobody but Simcoe would be gauche enough to call before eight o'clock. Except Brad O'Malley.

"Hi," Brad said with a bright smile. He looked vigorously awake. Freshly shaved, he was wearing a matched set of fawn shirt and cords. "I saw your bedroom light go on, and came to invite you to breakfast, since I didn't feed you last night."

"You sure know the way to a person's heart."

His eyes roamed over my turbaned head, the dressing gown, pulled taut across my chest, and the bare legs issuing beneath it. "You too. You do strange and wonderful things to that coat. That turban really suits you, Audrey. You look—regal," he said, fishing around for the right word. "Like Queen Nefertiti. It's the high cheekbones that do it."

"I'm not used to heady compliments so early in the morning. What do you serve a queen for breakfast—fish?"

"I didn't have any luck."

"After staying out so late, you came back empty-handed?"

"I'm sorry I bothered going." His steaming eyes suggested what alternative occupation would have been more enjoyable. "Come over as soon as you can."

He left, and I scrambled into my work clothes—a shirt and jeans—but I scavenged around till I found a pair of sandals to replace the open-toed moccasins. Delicious aromas filled the cottage when I went in. There was bacon sizzling, coffee perking, some tantalizing yeasty smell mingling with it.

I went to the kitchen door and said, "Can I help?"

He was just pouring some eggs into an omelette pan. "You can give those mushrooms a stir," he said.

While he finished the omelette, I buttered English muffins and poured coffee. We had a perfectly congenial breakfast, unmarred by bickering. Expansive from this royal treatment, I complimented him as we cleared the table.

"That was a feast. You're going to make some woman a great wife one day."

"The line forms to the right."

"I bet it does. How come you're not afraid to cook and clean, and do all those un-macho things?"

"Cooking isn't un-macho. The great chefs of the world are mostly men. Both men and women have male and female hormones," he said.

There were such things as bisexuals. This talk of mixed hormones almost sounded like a hint. "Did you have a sex-change operation or something?" I joked.

"Nope, I was born with my masculine appendage. Do you know what an appendage is, Audrey?"

"Sure. According to Webster, it's an adjunct to something larger or more important."

"Did you memorize the whole dictionary?"

"Appendage is a word that crops up in publishing."

"And sex. Being a man is just an adjunct to being a person. Persons have to eat, and some persons like to cook, too. They like nice houses, and when they outgrow the notion that only half the persons are allowed an interest in those things, they express that interest. The tail has stopped wagging the dog."

"An apt analogy." I grinned. He hit my rump with a spoon. "I guess it makes sense." I didn't say, but was aware that it took guts to act openly on his philosophy. "So you just do what you want—within the law, I mean?"

"The law's a crock."

"A cobweb that catches gnats, and lets the bumble bees fly right through."

"My law is not to hurt anybody."

"That's not *your* law. It's the Golden Rule. 'Do unto others . . .'"

"I've been trying. Don't you have any desire to do unto me?" He gave me a meaningful smile and said, "It wouldn't hurt you a bit to be nice to me, Audrey."

He was joking, but when I looked at him, our eyes held. I watched while his smile turned to a hopeful question. His arms reached for me. "The tail's beginning to wag the dog," he warned, as he pulled me into his arms, but slowly, giving me time to stop him if I wanted to.

It was a strange kiss—a gentle, tentative touching, then he pulled back and gazed at me uncertainly. When I tightened my arms around him, he stiffened for a noticeable minute before he crushed me against him and attacked vigorously. It was a small victory; I had made him stop and think, and something had overcome whatever reluctance that thinking had caused. After a long, bruising kiss, I pulled away.

He tilted his head and asked, "What brought that on?"

"I just felt like it."

"We must have breakfast together more often."

I could tell the instant the mood changed. The friendly intimacy was invaded by a gleam of the old leaping instinct. "Do you feel you know me well enough now to . . ."

"Not that well." I stepped back.

"This isn't the Victorian age, Audrey!"

"I really have to get to work."

"Is it something I said?"

"No."

"Something I didn't say—like 'I love you.' "

"I really have to go."

"You're running away."

"I'm only running next door."

"We'll have dinner together tonight," he called after me.

"I don't know . . . Don't put it like that. It sounds like a bribe."

"No strings attached! Honest."

"We'll see," I said, and fled from the kitchen. As I went through the living room, my eye caught something pink on the sofa table. It was a book. *Love's Last Longing*, it was called, and the name of the author was Rosalie Wildewood. There are books we admire, like *Pride and Prejudice*, and there are books we love, like *Gone with the Wind*. Anything by Rosalie Wildewood was a book beloved by me, and several million other red-blooded women, who had our fantasies graphically depicted in purple prose. We were saved from shame by the healthy dollops of history Rosalie provided. *Love's Last Longing* was her latest release. I picked it up and frowned at it, while Brad came trotting after me.

"What on earth are you doing with this?" I asked him.

"You recommended her. Idle curiosity. I just wanted to see what appeals to you."

He'd have a pretty weird idea of that if he were to judge by this book. At least I was assuming it would follow the pattern of Rosalie's other books. "Just bear in mind, what I read isn't necessarily what I enjoy doing."

"It's what you'd enjoy if you could let yourself go," he tempted.

"Maybe, but where would I find a pirate and a sea captain to do it with?"

"It's an emperor, and a prince."

"Oh, I haven't read this one. How'd you like it?"

"I'm just beginning. It seems lively, if contrived and overly dramatic."

"Kind of a female's version of Madison Gantry, would you say?"

"Something like that," he admitted. "Would you like to have it?"

"You're not finished."

"I picked up the latest Gantry too. Wildewood isn't really my style."

"You talked me into it," I said, and slipped it into my purse. "Funny—Rosalie Wildewood chose the same first name as Rosalie Hart. Of course it's fraught with romance."

"Audrey is beginning to sound like a wildly romantic name to me."

"Does Dane suggest anything? Other than the canine association, I mean? The Danes were fierce, you know."

"Blue cheese?" he said, and hunched his shoulders.

Funny an English professor hadn't said *Hamlet*. I went

home and put *Love's Last Longing* in the bedroom, away from temptation.

About fifteen minutes later, Brad jogged past my window. He'd changed back into his jogging outfit, and I knew his kitchen would be sparkling clean too. I wondered what he planned to make for dinner. Then I turned my attention back to my work and forgot Brad O'Malley for a whole ten minutes.

CHAPTER 5

The reason I thought of Brad was that I needed the diary he'd forgotten to return. He'd be jogging much longer than I could afford to wait, so I went over to get it myself.

I was surprised to hear the clatter of typewriter keys when I reached his door. He couldn't have jogged four miles already! Simcoe! He'd sneaked in around the back of the cottage so I wouldn't see him, and was checking for damages. But typing? Maybe the missis was with him. With a mischievous smile at the opportunity of catching them in the act, I quietly opened the door.

"Brad!" I exclaimed. There at the desk sat Brad, still in his jogging suit, typing away at sixty or seventy words a minute. "How'd you get back here?"

"Audrey!" He looked up, startled, and rushed to the door. The startled expression was tinged with guilt around the edges. "I took a short circuit today. Just looped around that little stand of cedars and came home. My leg's bothering me. I wrenched it last night when I was docking Simcoe's boat."

"You didn't say anything about it this morning."

He had his hand on my elbow, blocking the path to his desk. "It didn't act up till I tried to jog. What can I do for you?"

"I came for that diary of Rosalie's. The one about gaining weight."

"Have you got that far already?" he asked, staring.

"Not really. I'm listing various names and occupations of her lovers as a lure of what's to come. What are you writing?"

"I decided to jot down some ideas about Eliot—you remember we talked about it."

"You jot fast. You should get yourself an electric machine like mine. I thought it was the Simcoes in here, snooping around."

"No, just me. I'll get the diary." He went to his desk to get it. Funny it was on the desk, where he was working on the Eliot jottings.

"Thanks."

He didn't invite me in, or seem interested in casual chitchat. In fact, I had a distinct impression my intrusion was unwelcome. Subtle little things like opening the door and pushing me out before I mentioned leaving. "See you tonight," he called after me. "Dinner at seven-thirty—come early for a drink."

"Sure, see you."

"Would you mind bringing another of Rosalie's diaries? They make good light reading."

"Better than philosophy, huh? Sure, I'll bring one."

I forgot the visit as soon as I got back to work. It wasn't till the devastating phone call from Eileen that I remembered it. "Audrey, how's it going?" she asked.

"I should be done by the end of August—no problem."

"That's too late. The rumor is that Belton is a month ahead of us. Apparently Mason's sequestered himself somewhere and is writing like crazy. It'll knock a hundred thousand from our sales if he gets his out in time to cash in on all the excitement of Rosalie's death. Can you speed it up?"

"I'm writing as fast as I can. You know Mason's book will be a mishmash of old magazine articles, Eileen. I don't think he'll tap our market much."

"Let's be realistic. This isn't the Shakespeare audience we're after. Rosalie's fans will buy the first thing that comes along, and won't buy another a month later. Mason spices his up so well, you know, to appeal to the mass audience. Keep in touch. And about that illegitimate child, Audrey, see if you can pin it down. That's one item most people don't know about."

"There's nothing positive about it in her diary."

"Well, go through her letters with a fine-tooth comb. Maybe you could give that Lorraine Taylor a call."

"All that fine-tooth combing and calling isn't going to help my schedule."

"Do your best."

"Sure," I said, and hung up.

I hate you, Hume Mason, wherever you are. Panic had escalated to red alert, making work nearly impossible. I paced the room a minute to calm my nerves before going back to the typewriter. I bet Hume Mason had a word processor. How else could he pound out those execrable books so fast? Through the window, I glanced at Brad's cottage. It was a gorgeous day. Why wasn't he out working on his tan? Probably still in the cottage, typing away on his Eliot notes.

I wondered if those literary things paid well., He sure got a lot of money somewhere, with his Mercedes and his Guccis and his French restaurant. He couldn't possibly do all that on a professor's salary and a couple of academic essays. He must write something else as well. Maybe articles for *Playboy* or something, under an assumed name. Was that why he was in such an almighty hurry to get me out of the cottage this morning? Not that there was anything wrong with writing for *Playboy*. More power to him. Some of the top writers did it.

No, it must be something else. I remembered Rosalie's diary, there on the desk by his typewriter. I remembered his startled face when he asked if I'd got to that part already. *Alarm* wasn't too strong a word for his reaction. He was very interested in those diaries, in everything about Rosalie.

An unpleasant, niggling suspicion was scratching at the back of my brain. If he hadn't gone jogging today, who was to say he ever went? Maybe he just ran around the cedars and sneaked back home every day. Maybe he hadn't spent last night fishing either—the lights were on in his cottage, and he hadn't caught anything. Maybe he was in the cottage all the time, pounding away like a fiend at his typewriter. In a great hurry—to beat me! *He was Hume Mason,* holed up here in the country like me, to bang out his cheap, unauthorized book. He'd discovered somehow I was coming here with the research, and he came trotting after me. That's why the fashion model was living in a hovel! He was putting on this whole infatuated act to get at my research material!

The bastard! I glared at the cottage window. What an ass I was to have been taken in so easily. Bought with a couple of meals and a few kisses. I'd been seduced as surely as if he'd had his way with my body. I was beyond working. I couldn't think of anything but his trickery, and every detail bolstered my theory. His strong reaction when we heard of Rosalie's death—he looked like a zombie. He knew he had to get his book hammered out faster. And he even had the gall to ask me to bring another diary to him that night, to devour while I innocently slept, wasting time.

I ran back to my typewriter, but nobody could work when her adrenaline was pushing through her skull. My fingers were shaking with anger. I got up to go and confront him, then stopped at the door. He'd deny it, of course. He'd pull out that blasted dull book on Eliot and claim that was the source of his wealth. I couldn't prove otherwise, either, unless I used my wits. For that matter, I could be wrong. I was consumed with a desire to read what he was writing. I wouldn't let on I knew, but the first time he left his cottage, I'd go in and see for myself.

I forced myself back to work . His flashing eyes laughed at me between the lines. Every word he'd said came back to taunt me. He'd stood up for Hume Mason, intimated he was no worse than me when I put the man down. I knew there had to be a lead lining to my little cloud of pleasure. Well, here it was, raining pellets on me. For a few distraught hours, I'd write a line, then look to the cottage to see if Brad was leaving, reread what I'd written, and strike it out. It was hopeless. Nobody could write under these conditions. Barbara Cartland would run dry.

I phoned Lorraine Taylor, and heard she was in bed with a sedative. I went through the letters, trying to find some evidence that Rosalie had actually had a child, but there was nothing except that question about her feeling better. The word *nausea* was used. Morning sickness certainly caused nausea. I turned to the diary in which she'd mentioned gaining weight, and couldn't find even that passage. I knew I hadn't imagined it. I remembered mentioning it to Brad . . . and he'd borrowed that particular diary. That was the specific one he wanted. He'd removed the pages! I pulled the sheets back as far as they'd go, and sure enough,

two pages had been razored out, very neatly. So Hume
Mason was even going to have that coup!

It was suddenly noon hour, and I stopped for a can of
soup. Brad was probably simmering himself a duck à
l'orange. I was supposed to be having dinner with him
tonight. I wouldn't go, of course, but I'd let him waste a
few hours preparing it. I couldn't face a whole afternoon of
waiting for him to leave his cottage. I'd go as soon as I
finished my soup.

About two spoonfuls before that happened, he came to
my door. He didn't open it, but just called through the
screen. "I'm off to town to get some Grand Marnier for
dinner. Do you need anthing, Audry? Cigarettes . . ."

I kept my voice as close to normal as I could, to allay
suspicion. "I'm out of beer."

"I'll pick some up. See you at seven."

"You bet."

Through the screen I saw him back the Mercedes around
and fly down the road, leaving the inevitable cloud of dust
behind it. It was time to sneak into his cottage. Breaking
and entering was the official term for what I had in mind.
An indictable offense. But if it had been a capital one, it
wouldn't have stopped me; I was too mad.

As soon as he was gone, I darted to his cottage. The front
door was locked as tight as a drum. That in itself was
suspicious. I went around, checking windows, and found
the bedroom one wasn't impossible to lift. It wasn't easy
either, but by exerting all my strength, I finally moved it.
Scrambling in a window at chest level wasn't easy or
comfortable. I tore my shirt and scraped my legs through
the jeans, but at last I found myself on the floor inside the
cottage, headfirst.

I took a cursory look around the bedroom. A small
gold-framed picture of a woman on the beside table caught

my attention. At that point, I wouldn't have been surprised if it had been himself with a wife and kids, but it was only a woman. I recognized the sweetly smiling face. I'd been looking at it enough lately. It was a photograph of Rosalie, at the height of her beauty. Why would he have a picture of Rosalie by his bed, if not to imbue himself with her aura? He must have actually interviewed someone who knew her, and stolen the picture.

I hurried into the living room, heading straight for the desk, in hopes of finding the missing pages. A sheet of paper in the battered machine with neat, double-spaced typing on it caught my attention. My eye encountered no "prelapsarian" here, no "specious good." What I read with deep interest was "From the rim of her low-cut scarlet gown, a creamy bosom flowed gently as she came timidly toward him." The passage continued with many a throb and quiver, as the bosom was aided from the rim, molding itself compliantly to the warmth of his fingers, and engendering a shudder in his loins. Soon his manhood was swelling uncontrollably. I read on, till it—the manhood—was searing her vitals with a sweet sting. Despite her virginal timidity, she enjoyed the whole process to the point of ecstasy.

I was furious that he was fictionalizing Rosalie's sexual exploits with the breathless "I was there" quality and Day-Glo colors expected from Hume Mason. If this was a sample of his book, it was garbage, and would be snatched up by the thousands, leaving *Queen of Hearts* a mile behind.

A sheaf of pages was stacked beside the machine. With curiosity rampaging, I quickly looked through the sheets. There was no sign of the missing diary pages. It seemed to be Rosalie's affair with the judge he was writing, though the man's actual name wasn't on any of the pages. She called him "my darling" and he called her "you eternal woman." There was nothing like that in the diaries. Mason was unscrupulous, using every cheap trick in the book, and inventing a few of his own.

I took a quick look through the drawer for letters, hoping to get the scheduled publication date. Right in the top drawer there was a long envelope with the Belton Publishing Company name in the corner. I didn't hesitate a second before opening it. A Ms. Barlow was urging him on to the complete "the manuscript discussed by phone today" at top speed. No date was given, but the letter was dated two weeks before. Just time to learn that I was doing my book, and for them to discuss it by phone. The size of the advance staggered me. No wonder he drove a Mercedes. He could have driven a team of Rolls-Royces if he'd felt like it. Ms. Barlow had signed herself "Love, Vicki."

I rammed the letter back in the envelope, slammed the drawer, and gritted my teeth till I had stopped panting with anger. I did a quick sweep of the rest of the cottage, but couldn't find the diary pages. Even the kitchen—including the freezer, where I discovered a pile of frozen gourmet dinners wrapped up in aluminum foil and labeled. The ones on top were spaghetti Caruso—two of them. I had a pretty good idea what treat he planned to serve tonight, and let on he'd made it himself. He never took his head up from that damned typewriter, except to scatter rugs and tablecloths around the place.

I didn't know how long I'd been there, but the town where Brad was getting Grand Marnier wasn't far away, so I went back to the window and crawled out, landing in the scrub beneath on my hands. I couldn't get the window completely closed. I left it open an inch and ran home, with a look down the road to make sure he wasn't coming yet.

I sat on the lumpy sofa, hugging myself with my arms, as

though to keep in my body all the vituperation that was longing to spew forth. "I'll kill him. I'll kill him with my bare hands," I said two or three times, till the first wave of fury had dulled. "I can't believe I've been such an idiot."

Various revenges were plotted and rejected as too time-consuming. I wanted to write up phony diaries and expose Mason to lawsuits. I wanted to run back and burn his manuscript, to phone Eileen Haddon and demand more money, to sit down and finish my own book that same day and outdo him in pornography. Him and his ranting of helping me find a significant theme for my book! The *hypocrisy* of it— he just didn't want me to wander into his area of sleaze. In the end, I was too tired and defeated for any of these schemes. Mason was halfway through his book, if he was working chronologically. Chapters ahead of me. I opened a Coke, and wiped away the lone tear that trickled down my cheek. Mixed in with the rest was a regretful memory of my summer romance that never was, and never would be. He'd only found me "sensational" to get hold of my research. He thought I was a gullible dope—and he was right. First Garth, now Brad. Did I wear a sign on my butt that said "Kick here"?

It was blind luck that Eileen found out about Hume Mason. Eileen! I should phone her, but if I did, she'd urge me on to a faster pace, when I knew in my bones I couldn't write a word. Especially I couldn't compete with creamy, heaving bosoms and shuddering loins. I needed a very strong shock treatment. I put on my bathing suit, went down to the dock, and dove in, without even feeling the water first. It was every bit as cold as I remembered. I swam halfway to the island, then swam back and got out, panting, so numb that all sensation was gone from my body. Only my mind was active, as active as ever, and as frustrated.

I didn't wait till seven to call on Brad O'Malley. I saw his car under the tree when I went to my front door. With a towel wrapped around my waist like a sarong, I strode to the door and rapped sharply.

"Come on in," he called from the kitchen. "Hi, Audrey. Be right with you. The beer's in the frig. I'm just starting dinner. I hope you like chicken liver and pasta."

"Spaghetti Caruso?" I called back.

"Yeah, do you like it?"

He hadn't slipped the pans in the oven yet. No wild aromas pervaded the cottage this time. "Why don't you just take one of the frozen cartons from you freezer? I won't be joining you tonight."

His head peeked around the doorjamb. You never saw such a guilty-looking man. "Say what?"

"You heard me."

His body followed his head around the doorjamb. He wore a curious, confused look that turned to wariness when he got a look at me. "Is something the matter?" he asked.

"What could possibly be the matter? I'm fine. I'll be very busy. As you know, I'm writing an *authorized* biography of Rosalie Hart. I didn't bring along the other diary you asked for. In fact, I'd like you to return the pages you cut out of the previous one—you remember, the pages dealing with Rosalie's pregnancy. You'll have to make do with what you've already read, and that active imagination of yours. But then you wouldn't want to wreck your book with too many facts, Mr. Mason."

He advanced slowly into the room. In his hand he held a wooden spoon, and he wore an apron with a picture of a smiling chef on it. He looked bewildered. "Could you run that by me again in slow motion?" he asked, blinking.

"Run it out your ear. I know who you are, and I know what you're up to, and I want you to know I think you're disgusting and vile."

"Are we talking frozen dinners here?" he asked. "Listen, I really am a great chef. I made those dinners myself. I just took them out of my freezer at home . . ."

"I'm not talking about your lousy dinners! It's the reason for them we're discussing."

"Hey, no strings attached!"

I was panting so hard I could hardly talk, but I couldn't keep quiet either. "Look, I know you don't really like me. If a three-legged, bearded lady had had those diaries, you'd have been in there, wooing her with your frozen boeuf bourguignon and your Château de Snob. You must think I'm an *idiot*."

"Just unhinged," he smiled uneasily, and came closer, reaching for my arm. "Come and sit down. I'll pour you . . ."

I twitched away. "Alcohol isn't going to work either. And if you were counting on continued access to *my* research for *your* book, you can forget that too. I suggest you pack up your fancy car and trot your Madrid chair and your Cuisinart back to whatever rock you crawled out from under."

"That's 'Barcelona chair.' Listen, if you think I'm using Rosalie's diaries for a book or something, you've got it all wrong. That seems to be the gist of your tirade."

"Part of it, not the gist. The gist is that the masquerade is over, Mr. Mason."

"Mr. Mason?" he repeated dumbly.

"As in Hume, pornographer, sleazebag Mason. You can call Ms. Vicki at Belton and tell her you struck out. You'll have to move your ass and actually do some work yourself. You should be good at digging up dirt by now, you son of a bitch."

He actually had the nerve to smile! "Ah—you swear when you're mad. That's good. Relieves the tension. But I don't understand what you're mad about. Did I have a visitor while I was out? Did some phone call get misrouted to you? Where'd you get these crazy ideas?"

"Vicki didn't phone, or arrive in person. Funny you should think she had, when you claim to be ignorant."

"I *am* ignorant! *Innocent!* What I'm trying to find out is what put this bee in your bonnet."

"I had a revelation. A prelapsarian revelation."

"Sounds painful." He gave me a doubtful look.

"Bullshit!" I shouted in exasperation, and stormed out, clutching at my slipping sarong.

Just as I reached my door, Brad opened his and called after me: "Does this mean you're breaking our date tonight?"

"You figure it out, Professor."

A little later, as soon as he had got the frozen food into the oven, Brad opened his windows to let the fumes of spaghetti Caruso waft gently toward my door. I closed it. Actually the very thought of eating anything's liver turns my stomach, so it was no lure.

The confrontation cleared the air, and my head. I'd done the right thing to have it out. I went determinedly back to work and pounded the typewriter till my head ached. The adrenaline was flowing. Words magically strung themselves together into sentences, sentences into paragraphs, till I had five pages full—also one ashtray. After I emptied it, I opened the fridge for a beer, to reward myself. Then, after the store was closed, I remembered I was out of beer. I opened the door again to clear away the smoke, and was surrounded by the tantalizing smell of garlic and onions, oregano and chicken, which did not smell like livers at all. I closed the door again and made coffee, to drive away the other odors.

I turned on the TV and sat staring at the moving pictures,

without really seeing them. I looked at the phone, which
didn't ring; at the door, which was silent; then I looked
within myself for entertainment. There was only one
possible subject to consider, so I thought of it.

I'd shown him a thing or two. He must feel like two
cents, and the wretch didn't even have the manners to
apologize, or try to explain. You'd think he'd phone up and
say he was sorry at least. After all, we were both adults. I
didn't expect a man to be a saint. God, after Garth I didn't
expect much of men, but this went beyond even Garth
Schuyler's duplicity. There's some excuse for passion; this
was a coldly, carefully planned deception. It was Belton's
fault, for offering him so much money. It wasn't, though:
Belton hadn't told him how to get his research. Belton
hadn't told him to call me "sensational." Hadn't he meant
any of it? By nine, I decided that if he came suitably attired
in sackcloth and ashes, we might discuss the matter. There
would be no forgiving, but we could discuss. By nine-thirty
I realized the elegant Mr. Mason wouldn't be caught in
sackcloth, even if it had a Gucci label.

At nine thirty-five, he went to his car, wearing a
light-colored suit. A man didn't put on a suit to go out
alone, say to a drive-in movie. A suit like that was for a
date—maybe dancing. I felt as angry and cheated as if he'd
broken the date, instead of me. At least he wasn't writing
tonight. I had already worked past the saturation point, so in
a fit of boredom, I opened *Love's Last Longing*, and
became lost in the perils of an innocent child-woman
bearing the unlikely name of Melora with eyes of an
unconvincing turquoise shade. She was taken captive by a
Mogul emperor during some long-ago war.

I read till my eyes ached, marveling how Rosalie Wildewood could ever conceive of such a heroine, who juggled
the moon and stars with one hand, while the emperor

nibbled from the other. She nobly spurned his offer to wear the empress's crown, choosing instead to be a kitchen slave. Easy for Melora. She knew a prince was lurking in the next chapter. I wandered what he was like, and before I knew it, I was reading again. I literally couldn't put it down.

Lorraine Taylor didn't phone back. I went on hoping for quite a while, because of the time difference. When my eyes got too tired to read, I went down to the dock to look at the moon and the water. No emperor or prince sailed up to kidnap me. I must have been crazy to come here, out in the sticks, with nothing to do once the sun set. I drove into town and had a bottle of beer alone at a bar. I left half of it when some Neanderthal in a leather jacket tried to hit on me. I drove home by a circuitous route, in case he took it into his head to follow me. Brad's car still wasn't back. The Simcoes' curtains juggled, timing me in. Old Simcoe would be regretting this rift between us two red-hot lovers.

I wondered what Brad had said to him, to give him the idea we were an item. I felt suddenly frightened, alone in the cottage. I locked the door, but the Neanderthal from the bar, or someone like him, could get in without much trouble. I wouldn't go out alone again at night. But I'd make sure to get in a supply of beer and Coke.

I wanted to hear a human voice, and made the mistake of phoning Mom. She asked three or four times how I was, meaning was I suicidal about Garth and Helen. When I convinced her I was all right, she told me about some new wedding presents that people had sent. I told her the book was going fine, and no, I wasn't lonesome. There was a terrific guy next door. His name was Simcoe, I said. Eddie Simcoe. He was chasing after me so hard I couldn't get any work done.

"Jerome called," she said, as a crumb. Jerome Hespeler, literally the boy next door. A dear, sweet man, with less sex appeal in his entire body than Brad had in his little finger. He must have noticed my green complexion at the wedding. I'd give Jerome a call when I got back to New York. Safe, sexless men were beginning to seem a good idea.

CHAPTER 6

June 21, the first day of summer, and the longest day of the year. Why did I have to make it even longer by waking up at seven o'clock sharp? It was the crows yammering in the pine trees that caused it. Crickets chirping all night and crows all day—how was a person supposed to get any sleep? There was no background noise to mitigate the animal sounds either, no comfortable roar of traffic, no calming wail of a police or ambulance siren. I was definitely unbalanced to have come to this godforsaken spot. Still groggy, I padded into the kitchen to make coffee and let it perk while I showered and sorted out my day. Rosalie's funeral was this afternoon at three; that'd be six eastern time. It should be on the late news.

By seven-thirty I was at my typewriter, not knowing whether I was writing a high-class biography with a theme, or a poor imitation of Hume Mason quickie. Whatever else it was, it had to be fast, so I banged away, mindless of the nuances of style, mood, and tone; just getting down the facts, ma'am.

At eight there was a tap at the door. Probably Simcoe coming to tell me I was typing too loud, disturbing the

69

wife's vigil at the window. A scowl deepened to a glower when I pull the door open on Brad O'Malley. He was resplendent in a blue-and-white striped seersucker suit, all freshly shaved and combed, and smelling of whatever expensive scent he used.

"Whatever you want, the answer is no," I said baldly, and slammed the door. Or tried to.

He got the toe of his Gucci in it and pulled it open again before the lock caught. "You better wait to hear what I've got to say. It's not a request. I'm leaving."

"Good! If I'd had one wish, that would be it." My exclamation was loud and clear, and totally insincere. I felt as though the bottom was falling out of my stomach.

"Don't hire a band yet. I'll be back," he said grimly.

My stomach began rising again. "You can't win 'em all."

"I tried to figure out what you were talking about, after you left yesterday. You think I'm Hume Mason, right?"

"I *know* you're Hume Mason, Mr. Mason. Maybe you're Brad O'Malley too. I know if I wrote that kind of crap, I'd use an alias."

"Pen name is the word you're looking for. Pseudonym would do. Alias has a whiff of criminality to it."

"Thanks for the lecture, Professor. I'll stick to alias."

"Don't you want to hear why I'm leaving?"

"I never look a gift horse in the mouth."

"The reason I'm here is that I had a call from my wife last night. My son's in the hospital. Fell out of a tree, broke his leg rather badly. I have to go and see him." He examined me for traces of softening, and found instead a new rigidity.

"You neglected to mention there's a Mrs. Mason."

"We've been divorced for years," he said, dismissing wife, child, and marriage with a wave of his hand.

"I can believe that. The mystery is how you ever talked anyone into marrying you in the first place." This speech was accompanied by a wrestling match, during which I succeeded in shoving him physically out the door.

Once he was out, I went to the window to make sure he really left. He only took one of his Vuitton bags with him. With a quick glance at his Rolex, he hopped into his car and burned rubber.

A wife yet! A son——details too trivial to mention. He probably wasn't even divorced. And through all this mental abuse, the thought kept popping up, like a helium-filled balloon, bright and beautiful, that he was coming back. A half hour later, it also occurred to me that I hadn't found out where this wife and son lived. Probably in upstate New York, where he taught—if Hume Mason actually had time to teach between books that appeared with monotonous regularity, flooding book racks and driving out more worth-while books.

In any case, he wasn't abandoning his opus on Rosalie. This was some new scheme to fool me, but I'd outwit him. I'd beat him to print if I had to work night and day. Working was a good way to drive from my mind the image that haunted me: the perfect man. Physically perfect, that is.

Today should, by rights, have been only a minute or so longer than yesterday. It seemed to have about ninety-eight hours. Nobody could work for ninety-eight hours, so I had plenty of time to fret and fume. The arrival of the postman with a box of books for Mr. O'Malley, bearing the Belton label, didn't brighten the day much. Simcoe had apparently suggested leaving the box with me. I was surprised Mason had another book ready for release so soon after his Dean Mather story.

Surely this first day of summer should have been glorious weather-wise. Instead it started with a watery white sky in the morning, darkening to pale gray, and as the sun set, ominous purple-black clouds hung low over the river. A cold wind blew off the water. I imagined it originating in the polar ice caps, blowing across muskeg and prairies, picking up moisture from the river, before whistling in around the edges of door and windows.

It was downright eerie, being alone at night in a cottage in the middle of nowhere, with the wind battering the tall pines outside, occasionally tearing loose a branch that fell with a crack to the ground. Old Mother Nature was really in an uproar. When the rain began pelting the roof, lashing the windows and trickling in around the edges of the frames, I put on a sweater and wool socks, and was still cold. There wasn't even a fireplace to take the chill from the air. Who ever heard of a cottage without a fireplace?

I turned on the TV and watched a celebrity interview show. My interest was piqued when Rosalie Wildewood was one of the guests. She was doing a pitch of *Love's Last Longing*. She was as beautiful as any of her own heroines. Clouds of titian hair billowed around her face. "I'm a true romantic," she said. "Love is the lodestone of my life. A day without love is like a day without orange juice."

She looked surprised when the interviewer laughed, and offended when he suggested her love of love was extremely profitable. "It fills a need," she explained.

"What is your next book about?" he asked. She held *Love's Last Longing* up to the camera and launched into the tale of the ruined young heroine, the Mogul emperor, and the prince. "I mean the one you're working on now," he pointed out. It was a turn-of-the-century saga featuring a ruined young heroine, a judge, and a prince. The interviewer suggested the trappings changed; the heroine's trap, and the plot, didn't. Rosalie looked confused, but not offended. How did that beautiful nitwit write so well? She must be shy in front of the camera, I thought.

When the interview was over, I got my copy of *Love's*

Last Longing and settled in to read. Coffee would warm me.
I put a small pot on to perk, and rattled in the cupboard for
a mug. It was while I had the fridge door open that the
cottage was plunged into utter blackness, without any
warning. I yelped in surprise, then emitted a howl of dismay
as I realized what had happened. The power was gone, due
to the storm. And not even a candle in the place! Fear rose
insensibly to panic, till I remembered seeing a kerosene
lamp in the second bedroom. I twisted a sheet of newspaper
into a tight roll, lit it with my lighter, and went into the
bedroom. The lamp wouldn't have any fuel; I knew it as
surely as I knew the power would stay off all night.

Incredibly, it had two inches of pale liquid visible in its
dusty, transparent base. I lit the wick and dashed through
the dark cottage to dowse the burning paper in the sink. I
stumbled back through the dark for the lamp, put the shade
on, and went into the living room, trembling but relieved.
There's no reason to be scared, I told myself sternly. You're
no more likely to be attacked in the dark than with the lights
on. Except that it was so impenetrably dark out there, with
no streetlights, and no moon. A man could walk right up to
the door unseen. It was the Neanderthal in black leather
from the bar who came to mind. He wouldn't even have to
lurk behind a tree or bush.

A menacing rattle of thunder sounded in the distance,
followed by a ragged streak of lightning that, for one brief
instant, cast charcoal treetops into relief against the silver
sky. At least I wasn't one of those chickens who was afraid
of thunder and lightening.

There was really nothing to be afraid of. I'd just sit down,
read the book, watch some TV. Idiot! The power is off. All
right, sit down calmly and think. There, I think the rain is
letting up. It's not pounding as hard as it was. You haven't
read today's newspaper. If you put the lamp on the table and

the paper right beside it, you can see well enough to read. There was nothing in the paper about Rosalie Hart, and for me that summer, the wars in distant lands, the murders and rapes and other flowers of civilization had lost their significance. I flipped through the paper, but my mind was on my book.

Deprived of coffee, I went to the kitchen, lamp in hand, to get a glass of milk. Damn! Two inches left in the carton. If I drank it, I'd have to have black coffee in the morning, since the cream was gone. No beer. Last can of Coke then. I'd have to go into town tomorrow. I went back to the sofa and made a list: milk, beer, cream, Coke. It sounded like a liquid diet, so I added rye bread and apples. Maybe some oranges, for vitamin C. The trouble was, you had to eat the sour, messy things. If the lights didn't come on soon, I'd miss Rosalie's funeral on TV. Terrific, a perfect ending to this perfect first day of summer.

There was another roll of distant thunder, another flash of silver light, causing me to remind myself I wasn't afraid of storms. I wondered if Simcoe was out of power too, or if I'd maybe blown a fuse, in which case there wouldn't be any power till I replaced it. The best view of Simcoe's cottage was from my bedroom window. My tall form reflected in the windowpane, the light making me look like a picture of Florence Nightingale. There were two oil lamps burning in Simcoe's place. Back to the living room to add candles to my list, and a flashlight. The rain was definitely slackening now; it was hardly more than a patter. Or was that just water dripping from the trees?

I went to the window to check. It was impossible to tell, with so many rivulets racing down the pane. I leaned closer, and froze in that posture, staring, praying I was imagining it—that pair of eyes, not my own. A white moon of face floated in space, there at the window, just about level with mine. It was too dark to discern fine details. Black hair, a slash of shadow across the eyes—then it was gone.

I jumped back and let out a scream so high only a bat could appreciate it. For some seconds I stood still, everything but my vocal cords frozen solid with terror. It felt as if my very heart were still. My screams bounced off the walls, reverberated, rang. It was a few minutes before I could think. My first rational thought was of escape. My second was that to escape, I'd have to go out that menacing door, where he was. Probably waiting for me with an ax in his hand. Guns were too civilized for this wildnerness.

I thought of crawling out a window at the back, running over to Simcoe—but what if the man had run around to the back . . . I stood, trembling, too distraught to think straight. The telephone didn't so much as occur to me. When I heard the sound of a car on the road beyond, I ran to the kitchen window. The headlights wheeling right into the gravel path past my cottage made it impossible to see the car's make, but as it turned, I saw it was pale in color—white or beige or light gray. At least it was gone. I sat on the sofa till my heart settled down to normal, and the shaking stopped. Then, when the terror had passed, the lights came back on. Eager to share my story with someone, I phoned Simcoe.

"We were wondering who was calling on you at such an hour," he said. "We thought it was O'Malley, but when the car took off again so soon, we didn't know what to think," he admitted shamelessly. "It looked like two people in the car, but with the rain pelting so hard, the missus couldn't be sure. It was likely just somebody lost. People straggle down this lane from time to time, doing what they shouldn't. I wouldn't worry about it," he advised.

"You thought it was Mr. O'Malley's car?" I asked.

"Couldn't be sure. I haven't seen him since he took off

this morning. He didn't happen to say where he was going, when he was at your place?"

I nearly blurted out about his son, till I remembered Brad and I passed for sweethearts in this part of the woods. "A friend was hurt. He went to the hospital to see him, but he'll be back soon."

"It'd be best if he'd let me know he was going. I'd have kept an eye on the place for him."

"It came up suddenly—an accident."

I hung up and decided to make coffee after all, even though it was getting late, and I'd have to take it black. It didn't seem likely Brad was my Peeping Tom. Simcoe was probably right, was just a couple of amorous teenagers, lost in the storm. It was silly to get all nervous and jittery about it. I had real problems, without inventing imaginagry ones. Like my heart, for instance, which ached like a sore tooth. It felt actually physically heavy, causing my steps to drag. My jaw ached, too, from the strain of holding it up. It wanted to open wide and wail in grief.

By the time the coffee was ready, I'd missed the news, and Rosalie's funeral. I watched half the late show, till my eyelids began to droop and the commercials stepped up in pace. I switched the set off and went to bed.

My sleep was undisturbed throughout the night, in spite of the coffee, and the window peeker. Even when the burglar dropped a screwdriver on the uncarpeted floor, I didn't flutter an eyelid. I had no idea I'd been visited till I came out of my bedroom the next morning at seven-thirty, and saw the front door hanging open, blowing lightly in the breeze, just missing the screwdriver on the floor by an inch. I noticed that even before I saw I'd been robbed.

CHAPTER 7

"Oh my God!"

I stared at the large, empty table, where I'd left the box of diaries and letters from Rosalie beside my new type-writer. Everything was gone.

"My manuscript!" was my next spontaneous shout. Had he gotten away with it too? A week's work, gone without a trace. I ran around the room, trying to remember where I'd left the manuscript. Had I been reading it on the sofa? No—I'd made a list, read the newspaper. The manuscript had been sitting beside the typewriter. Gone then, the whole works. What else was missing? The TV was still there, a new color set less than a year old. Looking distractedly around, I noticed my polka dot nude painting was gone, and my heart shriveled in regret, but the more serious loss was the manuscript and the research. Anything else? Purse! Had he gotten away with my two hundred bucks in cash as well? No, thank God, it was on the sofa by the paper with my cigarettes and Bic. The wallet was probably empty. I rifled through it quickly—the money was still there. What kind of a burglar broke in and didn't touch a purse, sitting in plain sight?

I threw on my dressing gown and ran across the yard to Simcoe's cottage to tell my sorry tale.

"The prowler!" Simcoe said at once, his blue eyes sparkling in glee at this unexpected excitement. The wife wasn't in evidence. "I'll call the cops. I've asked them to keep an eye on us. They never pay a bit of attention. We're outside the town limits. It's the state troopers we have here."

A disembodied voice wailed in from the next room: "You'll want to put on some clothes if the police are coming." As Simcoe wore his usual blue shirt and trousers, I assumed this advice was for me.

"I will." I looked down and saw the mud on my bare feet, and the footprints in from the front door.

"I'll clean it up. She'll never know the difference," he told me with a conspiratorial wink.

I went home and got dressed. It took the police half an hour to come. Simcoe ran over as soon as he saw the cruiser pull up. I told them what had happened, and gave a list of missing items: my painting, papers and typewriter, with heavy emphasis on the manuscript and research. It had to be a literary theft, with the other things stolen to give it an air of ordinary breaking and entering. I showed Bucklin, the officer in charge, my full wallet to convince him.

Officer Bucklin had graying hair, a ruddy complexion, and a businesslike manner that didn't take kindly to the idea of anybody stealing a box of old diaries and letters.

"If you'll just give me the serial number of the typewriter, I'll get out a notice on it," he said.

"Actually it's the papers I'm more concerned about. And the painting for that matter. It was of a nude woman."

A condemning look raked me from head to toe, and he repeated, "The serial number, miss?"

"Serial number? I don't know. It was new—I can describe it."

He shook his head sadly. "What I need's the serial number. It makes it easier to get an ID. It'll be in a pawnshop by now."

"Was it insured?" Simcoe asked me.

"Insure a typewriter? No, it wasn't insured."

He and Bucklin shared another shake of the head.

"You ought to lock your doors at night," was the policeman's next piece of advice.

"The door was locked." I showed him where the entire mechanism had been unscrewed. The knob and lock were sitting on the floor. Simcoe flew over to assess the damage.

"That'll cost you." He smiled broadly.

"If there'd been a dead bolt on it, this wouldn't have happened," I retaliated.

"Can you describe the ve-hicle the man drove?" Bucklin asked. Once a cop learned to spell *vehicle*, he could never pronounce it right again.

"It was light-colored—that's all I saw," Simcoe told him.

"Who's in the cottage next door?" Bucklin asked, turning his questions to Simcoe. "He might have seen something."

"That tenant's away."

"It's odd they'd break into an occupied cottage, and not bother with an empty one," Bucklin mentioned. "They'd see by the car gone that the place was empty."

"They've likely cleaned him out too!" Simcoe exclaimed. He was nearly jumping for joy. "I've got the key right here. We'll go have a look."

"Would you know what he had in there?" Bucklin asked.

"Miss Dane can tell you. She spends half her time there," Simcoe said over his shoulder as he trotted to the door.

We crossed the wet grass and Simcoe unlocked Brad's door. "Do you notice anything missing?" Simcoe asked me.

I walked around the living room. It appeared to be intact. The kitchen, neat as a pin, contained all the unnecessary equipment I could remember. "It looks all right to me."

"Don't forget the bedroom," Simcoe said slyly.

I gave him a glacial stare. "I haven't been in the bedroom. Mr. O'Malley will be able to tell us if anything's missing when he gets back."

"Ask him to give me a call," Bucklin said.

"I will. But about the box of documents missing from my place—they're really *very* important. Irreplaceable. That's why I was robbed. Can you do anything to find them for me?"

Bucklin rubbed his neck and looked out the window. "Those items wouldn't be pawned, you see. They'll be kept privately. Who do you think would want them? And who'd know they were here?"

I explained about the other man, Mason, who was writing a book similar to my own, but was strangely reluctant to tell him Mason was O'Malley. There was enough bad blood between Brad and me without dragging in the police to make it official. Besides, I wasn't positive, and certainly didn't have any proof that would satisfy officialdom.

I gave the name and address of the Belton Publishing Company, and let Bucklin decide what to do about it. But whatever he did, I didn't expect to see my manuscript and research papers again. And how was I going to tell Eileen I'd lost them? It was a calamity—the end of my book, possibly my career. I'd never finish *Queen of Hearts* in time to satisfy Eileen, and I couldn't do a decent job without the precious diaries. The publisher wouldn't trust me after this fiasco. Oh lord, would I have to pay back the advance, already squandered?

After Bucklin left, I went back to my own cottage. The living room looked desolate, with the great empty table yawning before me. I'd loved that new typewriter too. It was a creampuff, gliding smoothly along at the lightest touch. Then I looked at the empty wall—my beautiful polka dot nude, another irreplaceable item. Worth even more, now that Rosalie was dead, but it was the sentimental loss that hurt. The hundred bucks spent on the frame pinched a little too. No insurance on it either, of course. I really had to get my life together. I bet Brad O'Malley had insurance on everything, and the serial numbers jotted down in a safety deposit box somewhere.

It had to be Brad who took the research. I'd cut him off, so the unscrupulous wretch had just plain stolen it. And taken the other things to confuse the issue. The visit to the injured son was an excuse to get away and arrange it all. He'd probably hired a cohort to do the actual theft. He wouldn't want to sully his own well-groomed fingers. That was why the man had been peeking in my window last night during the power failure, to make sure he had the right cottage, and that the box of papers was there on the table, where Brad had no doubt told him it was.

Eileen should be notified, but I wasn't eager to admit my stupidity and failure. I was half-grateful when Simcoe came pestering me about the broken lock. It gave me somebody to shout at. I even threatened to sue him for negligence. He went running home for his screwdriver and screwed the bits of pieces back in precarious place.

"What you ought to do is get yourself a chain for this door," he advised. "They've got them at Downes' Hardware Store in town."

"The horse has already bolted. Not much point locking the door now."

"There's still a filly in the barn." He smiled, showing his

moist, pink gums, sprinkled with an occasional remnant of tooth. Then he trotted back to confer with his own old gray mare.

Alone again, I tried to figure seriously how I could go on with the book, since I couldn't possibly repay the advance. I remembered the broad outlines of Rosalie's life, and who'd care about exact dates? But to start over from scratch! My contract didn't say August. October 1 was the date printed. I only *said* I'd try to do better. Well, dammit, I'd try.

I sat down and wrote lists of names, dates, events, films, trips—reams and reams of it, but just bare, fleshless facts. It was hopeless. In a fit of depression, I flipped on the TV to break the deafening silence. Even the crickets and crows were mute. It was the one bright spot in my day that the program was about Rosalie, and they were going to show film of her funeral. It was a half-hour show, beginning with a close-up of her star, embedded in concrete in Hollywood's Walk of Fame. One point of the star was broken, and I scribbled down this lone detail, which might possibly have eluded Mason. The film segued to cuts from her old films, stills of her various husbands. They didn't mention the painting that had occupied her last years. I looked sadly at the spot on the wall where the nude had lately hung. By God, I'd get that back from Mason, if I had to hire a detective to find out where he lived, and break in myself.

The last five minutes were about the death and funeral. Lorraine Taylor, the longtime companion who couldn't find time to return my call, was available for the cameras. She reenacted the death scene with enough relish to suggest she was a frustrated actress herself. Then the scene switched to the chapel, showing the casket borne by sedate pallbearers, a few young men included for their strong shoulders. The camera panned to the crowds waiting outside, a more than respectable showing, when you took into account that most of Rosalie's colleagues were already in their graves.

A few famous actors and actresses were among the mourning party that followed the coffin to the hearse, which would proceed to Forest Lawn Memorial Park for the burial. Lorraine Taylor was there, accompanied by a young woman holding her arm. That'd be Drew Taylor, Rosalie's daughter. She didn't look much like Rosalie, but she might take after her father. The camera shifted back to the chapel door as a starlet made her exit. My interest quickened. The man behind the starlet looked very much like Brad O'Malley. I held my breath, hoping the camera would move to him, but it went off to show a young girl sprinkling rose petals on the coffin.

The announcer said something about "a fitting end to a spectacular career that spanned three decades," and it was over. Of course it was Brad. He'd been in my cottage the morning of the funeral, but very early in the morning, and California was three hours behind New York. He could have made it to an afternoon funeral. Hume Mason's fat advance made it easy for him to hop a plane and garner details for his book.

But did going to California leave him time to plan the robbery of my research? He was out the night before, too, maybe not on a date after all. I pushed the thought away, to jot down, while it was fresh in my mind, a few notes on the funeral: the chapel name, burial site, my impressions of the crowd. I couldn't, or wouldn't, say they appeared mainly curious. They'd be pensive, forlorn, nostalgic when they got into print. Truth was fine, but there was a time for poetic license too, and giving a book a nice, weepy conclusion.

To be doing something useful, I started composing the closing chapter, with pen and paper. It was hard, since I was used to a typewriter. I looked up when a car scrunched the gravel on the road beyond the cottage. It pulled in next door, at Brad's place. I got up, curious to see who it was, not really thinking it was he. The white Mercedes glinted in the sun as Brad unfolded himself from the door, looking frazzled and hot and angry, with a lock of hair hanging over his forehead. He carried his jacket in one hand, and unlocked the trunk to pull out his bag. Before he went to his own cottage, he gave one long scowl at mine, but I was well hidden behind the curtain.

Some treacherous corner of my heart urged me to run out that door and go to him. It was an irrational, physical, instinctive thing. The anger still burned below, but it was quiescent now, diluted by the joyous lifting of my heart. I wondered with disbelief if I had gotten over Garth already. There was some vicious, insidious charm lurking in Brad's wrinkles. It lit sparks in his eyes, and entranced me, even when I was hating his arrogance and showing off. Just my luck to fall in love with a man I hated. I stood immobile, looking, waiting, with my heart revving in my throat, as though the day of judgment were approaching. Through the yellowing curtains made of some material akin to cheesecloth, I saw Brad's screen door open. He stalked out and came directly to my cottage. It took an act of concentrated will to turn my smile into a sneer of disdain.

Three imperative knocks sounded, and before I had time to answer, he wrenched the door open and stroke in, wearing a scowl. But it was an actor's scowl, which didn't quite conceal the wary light in his eyes. "I'm back," he announced.

"Whoopee! You should have notified me; I'd have had a brass band waiting."

"I see you haven't gotten over your snit yet."

"I was not in a *snit*. Snit doesn't begin to describe it."

The adrenaline started pumping at the memory of my problems, all of them caused by this man, who walked in as if he owned the place.

"I'd like to know what you're so fired up about," he said. His voice was rising toward a shout. There were traces of weariness about him in the wrinkled brow beaded with perspiration, the tie pulled down six inches from the collar. His trousers had lost their knife crease. These sartorial lapses appealed to my mothering instinct. My fingers wanted to soothe away the furrows in his brow.

"Use that hyperactive imagination!" I challenged. "It's your breaking into my cottage and stealing my manuscript and research for your book that I'm fired up about, Mr. Mason."

"Are you saying I'm that illiterate hack, Mason, again?"

"If the Gucci fits! And furthermore, I want my polka dot nude back, and my typewriter." Forgetful of the open windows and the proximity to Simcoe, my voice rose too.

His eyes widened and his mouth fell open at the same time, giving him an imbecilic expression. His glance flew to the empty table, the unadorned wall, then around the room to look for other losses. "What the hell are you talking about?" he demanded.

"Just what you think. You'd better hand them over, before I call the police."

"You mean you've been burgled and didn't call the cops?" He was dumbfounded.

"Of course I called them. They're looking for you right now. I might as well give them a buzz and tell them you're here. Unless you care to hand over my belongings?" I took a step toward the phone.

"I haven't got them. I haven't seen them. I'm not Mason," he said. His eyes glittered with a mixture of emotions, of which I suspect ill-natured joy made up some part.

I continued my march to the phone. "We'll let the police decide that."

He paced quickly after me and grabbed my hand as it reached for the phone. "Don't make a complete fool of yourself, Audrey. I don't know what happened here, but I was nowhere in the vicinity, and I can prove it if necessary."

"I already figured out you used an accomplice."

"I wonder if it *was* Mason?" he murmured, mostly to himself.

I shook off his hand and turned on him. "It was Mason all right. Who else would bother to steal my research?"

"From the glimpse I had of it, I could name half a dozen people. Supreme Court judges, presidential candidates, to name a few."

"They wouldn't steal my polka dot nude."

"Neither would Mason. Use your head, woman," he said impatiently. My blood started to simmer at this arrogant speech. "Why would Mason bother nicking a typewriter and a picture? Mason's loaded."

"That was to make it look like an ordinary robbery. Presidential candidates and Supreme Court judges wouldn't steal them either."

"What did the cops say?"

"They're looking into it."

"They might pick up the typewriter from the serial number. It'll turn up in a pawnshop somewhere eventually," Brad said.

"I can't wait that long. I need my things now, today."

"What's the serial number? I'll check out the secondhand dealers in the Yellow Pages and phone them to keep an eye out for it. It probably wouldn't be pawned right in town, but within a radius of fifty miles or so. They'd dump it early on, since it's bulky to tote around," he said, thinking aloud.

"I don't have the number," I mumbled.

"What did you say?"

"I said I don't have the serial number," I repeated, loud and clear. "I already told the police that."

Brad rolled his eyes. "That's a big help."

Frustration lent a rough edge to my voice. "Yeah, so are you," I said, and turned away to hide the moistening of my eyes.

After a little pause, Brad came up behind me. "Are you all right?" he asked doubtfully.

I ground my teeth and assured him I'd never been better. Encouraged by this irony, he put an arm around me and patted my head. What he really wanted to see was whether I was crying, so I blinked away the tear. "I'm sorry," he said. "I shouldn't have ripped up at you. You must be very upset. I know how much this book means to you."

His touch was gentle, his voice sympathetic. At his touch, I felt a wave of self-pity rise up to engulf me. "I'll get over it." Unfortunately my voice broke, and I emitted a hiccoughing sound. He peered down at me. "I'm not crying!"

"Why don't you sit down and tell me all about it—everything, just the way it happened." He urged me toward the sofa. "You can start with ransacking my cottage, or better, what made you decide to do it."

We sat down, holding hands, and I went over the doings of the past few days, starting with the call from Eileen about Hume Mason, and going on to my suspicions of his borrowing my diaries, and typing busily when he was supposed to be out jogging, and of course my discovery in his cottage. It felt good to get it off my chest. When I was done, I waited for his apology.

"You should have told me! It's all so simple really," he assured me with a rueful smile. "You knew I was a fan of Rosalie's. I found the picture in an antique shop. It was the frame that first caught my attention. It's lovely—you must have noticed. Antique French. It seemed like fate that Rosalie's picture was in it, so I left it in. It got packed and sent here by accident when the movers brought my things from the apartment. Since I was reading Rosalie's diary in bed, I put the picture on the table, to visualize her more vividly. That's all." He smiled innocently and looked to see if I swallowed this claptrap.

"What were you typing that day, that stuff about the creamy bosoms flowing out of the red dress? You had Rosalie's diary there on your desk."

A hint of embarrassment flushed his cheeks. "I was asked to do an article for one of the men's magazines."

"Which one? *Playboy*?"

"The other one," he admitted sheepishly. "They asked me to do an article on Rosalie. I got a phone call the very night she died."

"When did you have your phone installed? I didn't see the Bell truck there."

"I had Simcoe arrange it before I came here. It's just an article I'm doing. It won't be competition for your book."

"But there was nothing like that in her diaries."

He gave a little betraying lurch, but soon recovered. "I was describing her in *The Girl From Lovesick Lake*. Remember that one?"

"I don't remember a red dress. Her movies were all black and white."

"Artistic license. It's easier to visualize if you throw in an appeal to the senses. And since Freud, we all know that red symbolizes."

"She wouldn't wear a red dress with her orange hair. So

you really *did* go to see your son yesterday? How is he?" I felt the stirring of compunction that I hadn't asked this earlier.

"He's okay. It was just a green fracture. My wife—ex-wife—is excitable. I pictured an amputation or something awful."

"You never mentioned your son before," I said leadingly, though it was tacitly understood that it was the mother who was of more interest.

"What is there to mention?" I waited while my demanding eyes urged him to continue. "We got married nine years ago," he said reluctantly. "Within six months we both knew it was a mistake, but by then Sean was on the way, so we stayed married till he was born. Sean's the only tie between us now."

"So Sean's eight years old?"

"Yeah, a cute little guy. I wish I knew him better." His handsome wrinkles lent a vulnerable air to his plight.

"Does he live far away?"

"In Pittsburgh, with his mother and stepfather. My wife got custody."

"What's her name?" What I really wanted to know was what she was like in appearance and personality, but he seemed loathe to discuss her.

"What difference does all this make, Audrey?"

"Humor me."

"Her name's Helen Schaeffer now, but we have more important things to talk about," he said, with an air of finality.

The single word *Helen* imbued his ex with every possible attraction. "Yes, I'd like to talk about that article you're writing. What do those magazines pay, Brad?"

He mentioned an exorbitant figure. Other things bothered me too. Like the letter from Belton Publishing Company, asking him to hurry up his manuscript. And as I thought about the pages on his desk, they didn't sound like an article on Rosalie, but like parts of a sensational-style book. Brad was making noises about finding my material, but what better way to make sure I didn't find it than to lead me off on a wild goose chase? I didn't think he'd been to Pittsburgh either. The man in the crowd at Rosalie's funeral looked exactly like him. While he researched the funeral and gave himself an alibi, he could have hired men to break into my cottage.

I adopted a sympathetic pose. "You must be exhausted, Brad. Jet lag's a killer. I bet it was as hot as hades in California too," I added nonchalantly, and patted his hand to distract him.

His fingers curled over mine, and he smiled peacefully. "A hundred deg— *California*?" he asked, in a loud, guilty voice.

I pulled my hand away and stared at him. "You looked great on TV. Did you get all the details of the funeral for your book?"

"Audrey!"

I rose and stood, arms akimbo, to hear what he had to say. He thought for a revealing moment, then counterattacked. "You've been leading me on. You didn't believe a word I said."

"I didn't happen to be born a cretin."

"Appearances to the contrary!"

This conciliatory speech really tore it. "I'm going to call the police."

"What are you going to tell them?" he taunted. "That your nasty neighbor called you names?"

"No, that he broke into my cottage and stole some things."

"Must be a thief at large in the neighborhood," he said

pleasantly. "I have a little breaking and entering to report myself."

"I didn't take anything!"

He hunched his shoulders. "Nobody said you did. But there was a hundred bucks missing from my dresser."

"I didn't *steal* anything!"

"Gee, I hope you didn't leave your fingerprints all over that window you crawled in, and forgot to close."

"You knew all along. You put me through that confession, and all the time you *knew*."

A triumphant smile flickered. "*I* wasn't born a cretin either."

"Snakes aren't born; they're hatched."

His smile broadened to a hateful grin. "So are turkeys."

As I turned to stomp into the bedroom, my eyes happened to fall on the box of books from Belton, left by the postman. I picked it up and pointed to the Belton label. "Why don't you open this box and show me what Belton sent you, Brad?" He grabbed the box as if it contained dynamite that might blow up in his face. "Well, what are you waiting for? If you're not Mason, there's no reason Belton would be sending you copies of his latest masterpiece, is there? Why don't you just open it, and prove I'm wrong."

"You *are* wrong. I review books for Belton. These are review copies."

"Eliot—Popper—Hume Mason?"

"They send me lots of prerelease books. There might be one copy of a Mason book in here," he admitted.

"I'd say at a guess there are the usual twenty PR copies."

He put the book on the table and stuck his thumbnail into the tape. I waited with held breath to see what was in the box. He looked at me, frustration filling his eyes and carving ridges from his nose to his lips. Then he drew his hand back from the tape, picked up the box, and said, "No,

I don't have to prove anything to you. I'm telling you there are no Mason books in here."

"Maybe just one, to be reviewed by the illustrious Professor O'Malley," I reminded him.

He looked as if he wanted to strike me. "You just don't quit, do you?" he growled. And he stalked out the door, with his box of Mason books under his arm.

I noticed he didn't take them into his cottage, but locked them in the trunk of his car, to be certain I never got a look at them. Then he got into his car himself, revved up the motor, and took off. He looked mad enough to be going to the police. That was all I needed, to end up in jail for having tried, most ineffectually, to defend myself against a viper. Why hadn't I opened that box before he came?

I was too honorable—that was my trouble. I should have burned his manuscript when I first found it. I *must* be a cretin to have listened to his song and dance about a son with a broken leg. He'd been in California. He was guilty of everything I suspected him of, and to top it off, I was the one who might end up in court.

CHAPTER 8

The last thing I expected was that I'd ever get my stolen items back. At four-thirty, Brad's car returned, and soon he came stalking over to my cottage. I thought seriously about not letting him in, but was curious to hear whether the police were following him to arrest me. They'd break down the door and I'd owe Simcoe for damages. I opened the door, and had my typewriter thrust into my arms by a scowling Brad O'Malley.

"The cops found it at the incinerator," he said tersely.

I staggered under the weight of the machine. "The incinerator? What was it doing there?"

"It didn't say." When he noticed I could hardly hold the weight, he took the machine from me again. "I'd guess whoever took it decided to dump it. He didn't want to risk getting caught by selling it. An old wino was rooting in the rubble and found it. He brought it into the station, hoping for a reward."

"Oh, I'll pay him! This is great luck." I steered Brad to the table to deposit the machine.

"I gave him ten bucks. That'll let him celebrate in style. He was at the station when I got there."

I stole a peek at his profile. "I suppose you went to report me?"

He looked up and shook his head ruefully. "Who do you think I am, the Marquis de Sade?" I held back my own theory; Hume Mason. "You've got enough troubles for both of us. Come on," he said, and took my hand.

"Where are we going?"

"To the dump, to look for the rest of your stuff. The police sent a rookie down, but I noticed his hands and shoes were clean when he came back. I don't think he did a very thorough job."

"I'll jot down the serial number before I go."

"They already have it at the station. Come on, before it gets dark." I grabbed my purse, he grabbed my hand, and together we headed for the door.

"Why are you helping me?"

"It's pretty clear you're never going to get that damned book finished if I don't help you. Mason's probably more than half-done by now."

I gave him a sharp look. "Probably?"

"Let's not go into that again."

"Okay, we'll put it on the back burner. This is my maiden trip in your car," I mentioned as we slid onto the leather seat.

"So far I've just run your errands, without the pleasure of your company. How do you like it?"

"It's nice. I always buy American myself, to help out the unemployment." He ignored this pious put-down and rocketed along the lane to the highway.

The local dump was down a side road. Curls of blue smoke that smelled like burning rubber gave advance warning before we reached the gate. We got out and stared in dismay at a small mountain range of smoking garbage, whose disintegration was hastened along by a dilatory, smoldering fire. The EPA couldn't be aware of this.

"You should have changed out of your good trousers," I said. The Guccis should have been replaced by rubber boots too, but there was no way Brad would own anything so plebeian.

"We could do with a pair of gas masks, too," he added, lips curling in distaste.

He bent down and rolled up his trousers. "Come on. Hold your breath and let's get started. They said the typewriter was at the foot of the biggest pile. That'd be Mount St. Helens there in the center."

To actually scale that mountain of smoking rubble was a daunting task. Broken bottles and tin cans oozed from split garbage bags. There were papers and old clothes, shoes and skates, along with the more usual remains of food.

As the acrid fumes and stench seeped into my throat, I said, "This is a high price to pay, even for my research."

"Are you suggesting we quit?" he asked hopefully.

"Certainly not!"

"How about your picture, the nude? It'd be the easiest thing to spot if it's here."

"Let's have a look."

He took my hand and we advanced to the foot of the mountain. Brad took a deep breath, held it, and leapt up the garbage pile, as agile as a goat. He got up three or four steps, pulling me behind him, before his loafer slipped on a grapefruit skin, and he sank ankle-deep in garbage. I crawled more carefully behind him, coughing and batting at the smoke with my free hand. The mountain wasn't hot, but it was warm.

"Wrap this around your nose and mouth," he said, and handed me a folded handkerchief. It didn't cut down on the vile inhalations. The smoke seeped up under the mask.

From midpoint up the mountain, we could see to the top, and there was no sign of my belongings. We plodded slowly to the other side, slipping, sliding, many times having to steady ourselves by putting a hand on the garbage below. "You know, we *are* both cretins," Brad said, when we stopped to rest.

"Speak for yourself. For me, this is a matter of life or debt."

"No, I mean your stuff wouldn't be this high up on the hill. The dump trucks reach these heights. Some guy throwing a box wouldn't get it higher than a few feet off the ground. I'll slide down first and catch you."

He slipped and slithered down, balancing himself by stretching his arms out. He had nearly reached the bottom when he stepped on a slippery plastic bag and went sprawling in the garbage. The force of his fall sent puffs of smoke billowing from among the plastic bags and loose refuse. When he picked himself up, the seat of his trousers was decorated with a banana peel and coffee grounds. I bit my lip to hold back a laugh. He turned to help me down, our arms reaching out to each other in a grotesque parody of some TV perfume commercial. I got to the bottom without incident.

"Let's use sticks to poke around," I suggested. I found a long black umbrella, and Brad armed himself with a hollow aluminum tube. We poked and prodded our way around the first mountain, overturning any cardboard cartons of approximately the proper size.

"A lot of people throw their garbage out in cardboard boxes," I mentioned, after poking open the ninth or tenth carton that looked like mine.

"I'll take the hill on the left, you do the right," Brad said. It was obvious by then that the larger hill held nothing of interest to us.

After a few minutes, he called, "Hey, Audrey! Look at this!"

My heart raced with hope as I cantered to his hill, to see him holding an alarm clock. "It works. Is it yours?" he asked eagerly.

"I never saw it before in my life. You might as well come down." I pulled down the bothersome handkerchief and gave a disheartened sigh. "We're going to catch hydrophobia here."

"Want to split?"

"*I* can't leave till I'm *positive* my things aren't here, but if you want to . . ."

He cocked his head to one side and looked discouraged, but his words were cheerful. "I'll tell you what, let's keep our eyes peeled for the gilt frame of your picture, and if we find it, we'll look around that area for your box and manuscript."

"I bet Mason has my research, and this is a waste of time."

"You're the only one who thinks Mason has it. I happen to feel Mason has nothing to do with it. Don't ask. Just keep looking. If you can't stand the stench, get out of the garbage dump. You wait in the car."

"I had no intention of quitting! I just thought maybe you wanted to."

I took a long, hard look at him. He was Mason, and if he didn't have my research, then this was the likeliest place for it. "I'll go back to the other hill." For another fifteen minutes we worked, finishing our respective mounds, and poking about in the debris. There was a large area of litter surrounding the piles of garbage.

"There's a box that didn't quite make it to Mount St. Helens," Brad said, and rolled a brown carton over with his metal rod. It flew open, and one of Rosalie's diaries tumbled out on the ground.

We looked at each other in delighted disbelief; then, laughing, we scrabbled in the box to make sure we weren't hallucinating.

"It's here! Everything's here!" I squealed, incredulous. "Look, he even stuffed my manuscript into the box. All covered with oil or something where it fell out. Isn't it wonderful!"

I held the mangled pages out for his examination, but he wasn't looking at them. He was smiling fatuously at my dirty face, and the egg yolk rapidly congealing in my hair.

I was overcome with gratitude and remorse. "How can I ever thank you, Brad?"

His eyes steamed softly into mine. "I'll think of something," he warned.

We stuffed the papers back into the box and Brad carried it to the trunk of his car, where he deposited it right beside his carton from Belton, which we both chose to ignore, at least verbally, though we exchanged a meaningful look.

"Why would anybody have stolen it, only to throw it all away again?" I wondered.

Brad shook his head in confusion. "It's the damnedest thing I ever heard of. Worst thing I ever smelled too. I don't envy you, having to work with this."

"I'll have to retype the whole thing."

"Put a sheet of glass over it, or you'll be asphyxiated."

"Maybe I could photocopy it."

"I'm going home to soak for about ten days, and burn every stitch I have on." We rolled down the car windows and were off.

"I may never eat again. This gives me a whole new perspective on food," I declared.

"We got everything back but the picture," Brad said as

we sped down the bumpy road. "I was sure that was the first thing we'd find. It should have stuck out a mile."

"He may have ripped off the frame, but even the picture would be highly visible. It wasn't there, or we'd have seen it. I wonder if that wino . . ."

"No, I asked him. He was sober enough to understand. If he'd seen it, he'd have been willing to sell it back for another ten bucks. In fact, I wouldn't be surprised if he meant to come back and have a look for it himself. It begins to look as though somebody staged the whole robbery just to get the picture," he added pensively. "I didn't think it was that hot myself."

"You prefer your nudes with staples in their belly buttons?"

"You're out of date—they overcame that months ago. It was an interesting picture, but hardly a masterpiece. An original Pissarro would be worth a fortune, but a Rosalie Hart copy of a Pissarro—I wonder what that's worth, now that she's dead."

"A thousand or so I guess, for sentimental value."

"Some demented fan may have stolen it. You read about lunatics pestering the stars."

"Not usually such faded stars as Rosalie, and besides, hardly anybody knew I was here. Why wouldn't he keep the diaries too, if he was that infatuated with her?"

"So we're back to your original question. Who'd steal your stuff, just to take it to the city dump? And why did he keep the picture?"

"I don't know, unless he's so ignorant he thought it was a valuable masterpiece."

"In which case he was no art thief. An ordinary, garden-variety thief would have stolen your wallet while he was at it."

"What we have here is a mystery wrapped in an enigma," I decided. But I was too relieved to be despondent.

When we reached the cottage, Brad left the box on my porch to allow the stench to dissipate before taking it inside. I examined it thoroughly; everything was there. Across the yard, Mrs. Simcoe's curtain twitched busily.

She was getting an eyeful this time. "I wonder what she thinks of this," I said, and laughed. Brad's once-beautiful shirt looked like an artist's rag. There was a smear of some red goo down one sleeve, ketchup or spaghetti sauce. Various brown, black, and green stains were splattered at random across it, and down the trouser legs. The Guccis no longer shone like new pennies, but were sodden and caked in grime. His hair was disheveled, and his face was streaked where he'd wiped the sweat away with dirty hands.

I knew I looked as bad, but then I'd never aspired to his heights of fashion. Some few images in life are indelibly etched in memory: our mothers, the bedrooms we grew up in, our first lovers. I knew I'd added one of these precious pictures to my mental album. I would never forget the sight of the impeccable Brad O'Malley falling on his keister in the garbage dump, surrounded by the smoke of putrefying refuse.

"Penny for your thoughts," he said, watching me watch him. A little smile lifted his lips, and creased the corners of his eyes.

"This one's not for sale."

"She probably thinks we were mud wrestling."

"What?"

"You wondered what the missus thought of our condition," he reminded me.

"Oh—yes, if she can't think of some worse construction to put on it."

"I want you to know, Audrey Dane, I wouldn't have done this for just anyone." His eyes were steaming again as he gazed at me.

"I know," I said, over the lump in my throat. "Thanks, Brad."

"It was a pleasure. No, I'll rephrase that: I was happy to do it for you."

The words were trite, but the moment seemed tinged with a fairy-tale quality reminiscent of heroes slaying dragons for the princess. And at that instant, Brad, filthy clothes and all, looked like a perfect Prince Charming. This wasn't the arrogant professor who read me lectures on poetry or word meanings. It wasn't the macho male seducer who occasionally lunged at me. It was a thoroughly nice man. The lump in my throat grew, and before I could stop it, I felt a rush of hot tears.

He lifted a gentle finger and brushed one away. "I must be dowsed in onions," he said. There was a hoarse edge to his voice. He was feeling it also, then, this wave of tenderness.

"Ketchup too," I said, wiping at the smear on his shirt. His arm felt strong and warm beneath the cloth. I felt it tense at my touch. "All the fixings for a hamburger."

I expected some clever, bantering answer. Brad looked suddenly serious—more than serious. He looked sober. "Audrey, I'm sorry!"

I was not only surprised but confused. "For what?"

"Ah, I've been acting like a jerk," he said. "Lying to you about the diaries I borrowed, and that crack about reporting you for breaking into my cottage. Pretending I cooked those dinners."

"I haven't exactly been Pollyanna myself. I'm not usually so—"

"Hostile?" he suggested helpfully.

"Have I been hostile? I was going to say temperamental."

"Close enough. So, are we friends?"

"Friends."

We shook hands. But there are handshakes, and handshakes. This one was a very warm handshake. Our fingers clung lovingly while we gazed into each other's eyes. If Simcoe hadn't come out to rake the mud patch in front of his house, I think it might have escalated to something more.

"I'm going to have a marathon shower, then we're going out for dinner," he said.

"It's my treat. I insist. It's the least I can do."

His sober mood faded and a mischievous grin peeped out. "Don't feel obliged to do the *least* that courtesy demands."

"You can't be nice to some people," I groused, and pretended to be annoyed. In fact, my hormones began twitching, as he went on gazing at me.

"You can be nice to me anytime you want."

CHAPTER 9

Between finding my research all intact and being on speaking terms with my neighbor again, it felt like Christmas in June. Of course a few stray questions still bothered me. Like, was he or wasn't he Hume Mason? If he was, why had he helped me find the research, and if he wasn't, what was he doing with that box from Belton in the trunk of his car, to say nothing of the letter in his desk urging him to complete his manuscript? If he wasn't Hume Mason, what was that pile of literary rubbish doing beside his typewriter? You'd wouldn't think a professor with a fine reputation would write that kind of junk. Then I remembered the advance mentioned, and Brad's expensive life-style.

He certainly wrote something unbecoming to a professor of literature, and he wrote it for Belton. Belton seemed to have cornered the market on best-sellers recently. They had not only Hume Mason, but Rosalie Wildewood and Madison Gantry and . . . *Madison Gantry*!

My God, that was it! He was Madison Gantry! I laughed out loud for relief and joy. All his modest praise of this writer came back to me. "Gantry isn't quite as illiterate as most of the escape writers." I dropped my filthy clothes and moccasins in a garbage bag and tied the top in a knot so I wouldn't have to touch any of it after my shower. Or better, a long soak in the tub, with a copy of Madison Gantry's *Pavane for a Polish Princess* to keep me company. All his titles used alliteration and some musical term. Brad was interested in music, and alliteration would come naturally to a poetry critic.

It was a very enjoyable soak. I knew who had written the book as soon as Max Gerter, the hero, who happened to be an ex-professor of literature, began preparing spaghetti Caruso in chapter three. Before long, bosoms were flowing all over the place, hearts were throbbing, pulses were quivering, and loins were shuddering. There was no doubt in my mind who had written it. The only question now was why Brad had wanted my copies of Rosalie's diaries, and what that one had been doing on his desk, when he said he was writing an essay on her. Maybe he really was an innocent fan—he had her picture on his bedside table. But was he so keen a fan that he went to her funeral? It must have been Cary Grant's younger brother. There was one other question too, but I had an inkling of the answer to it. Why hide that he was Madison Gantry? Stupid pride, which boasted of that sedative of a book on Eliot, made him ashamed of these detective stories.

I was in an expansive mood. I wouldn't admit I'd discovered his secret, but I'd tell him I'd read *Pavane for a Polish Princess* and loved it. I'd praise the literary touches of Max Gerter, the detective hero. I wondered why he'd made him of German extraction, instead of Irish. Maybe he wanted the cool, assessing Teutonic mind in his hero, and not the amiable sort of romantic Celt associated with Ireland. The hero's mind may have been cool and assessing, but the book was wildly romantic, in the true sense of the word. It was a work of passion rather than reason. It was

funny and witty and very cleverly done. Madison Gantry
gained a fan; I planned to borrow every one of Brad's
books. In fact, I'd pay the ultimate compliment, and
actually buy them.

As the shadows grew long and the water grew tepid, I
took a quick shower to wash my hair, and bundled myself
into a towel. The evening nip in the air made it feasible to
wear the one good outfit I'd brought with me. Carefully
hung in the back of the closet in a plastic cleaner's bag was
a white shantung suit with a designer label, which I'd
planned to wear when I took my manuscript to New York,
sealed and ready for acceptance. I fully expected a first-rate
lunch with Eileen to celebrate the occasion.

Aware of the high standards of Max Gerter's ladies, I
surveyed myself closely in the mirror. The sleek lines of the
jacket suited my lean body. It clung to my meager curves,
and the slit in the skirt showed a generous length of leg.
While my hair was still damp, I took advantage of its
tractability and pulled it into a swirl on the back of my head.
Gold hoop earrings and the gold chains were added to ears
and neck respectively. A frivolous scarlet handkerchief
stuck into the jacket pocket added a touch of color. We all
know what red stands for.

A few sessions in the sun had removed the slug-like
pallor from my skin, and anticipation of a wonderful
evening brightened my eyes. Didn't I wish Garth could see
me like this! I decided, with an unaccustomed fit of
confidence, that I looked a suitable date for Brad O'Malley.

Just why he chose that particular evening to appear in a
cambric shirt, blue cords, and brown hippie sandals was not
yet clear. I'd told him the best dinner money could buy.

"Did you think I was going to take you out for a
hamburger?" I asked.

"A class act, Audrey," he approved, looking me up and down. "I'll run home and pick up a jacket."

A jean jacket wouldn't add much to his outfit, and anything else would look silly. "No hurry."

"Right, I'll put on a tie and get out of these sandals."

I waited for him at his car. He was back in minutes, much better dressed for the evening I had in mind. The Mercedes had been not only aired but taken to a car wash while I soaked in the tub. It shone dully in the glow of twilight.

"There's a good restaurant down at the bay, where we can dance on an outdoor patio," Brad said. "Do you want to give it a try?"

"It sounds fine. I haven't done much scouting since I've been here."

The dining room looked over the river, across the dance patio, where potted plants and flowers lent an exotic air. The maître d' greeted Brad by name. "They have rooms to rent. I stayed here one night," Brad explained.

Our table had a choice view. The cocktail waitress wore a brief outfit that showed fire-engine-red briefs beneath a short ruffle of black skirt. A busty redhead, she said, "Good evening, Mr. O'Malley," and gave him a big smile when she came to take our order. "The usual?"

"The usual for me, Marnie. What'll you have, Audrey?"

"I'll try your 'usual' too." I was expecting a glass of Château de, but got a double martini. "Marnie has a good memory. How long ago did you stay here?"

"Just a week ago, before I went to Simcoe's place. I stayed a couple of nights actually, while I looked around for a quiet spot to spend the summer. It's nice here. They have tennis courts, a pool, a boat tour of the Thousand Islands. It was Marnie who put me on to Simcoe. She lives near there, and commutes to work here."

Brad smiled an intimate smile across the table. "Little did

I know at the time that it would all work out so beautifully. You look fantastic in that getup, Audrey. I thought you liked a more casual style. I was trying to suit myself to you." I was flattered by his thoughtfulness, and admitted I had been trying to match him.

"You don't have to change anything for me. You're pretty terrific just the way you are." His voice was a caress; his eyes glowed with admiration.

Marnie came jiggling back with the dinner menus. I pressed Brad to have the surf and turf, since that was the most expensive thing they served. Over dinner, I wanted to extol Madison Gantry's genius, but Brad kept detouring me to talk about the theft from my cottage, and the mystery surrounding it.

"Did you lose much writing time? How long do you figure it will set you back?" he asked.

"A few days. I can make it up."

"I'll retype anything that needs retyping. You're sure everything is there, in the box?"

"Positive. The box hadn't even been rifled. I think he just opened the lid and rammed in my manuscript. Weird!"

"It confirms you weren't burgled for your research or the typewriter. What he did take and keep was the polka dot nude."

"It sounds like a case for Max Gerter. I'm reading *Pavane for a Polish Princess*, by the way. It's terrific. I'm really glad you put me on to Madison Gantry."

"Yeah, he's good. You know, I keep wondering why someone wanted that nude painting. It's not worth a lot in dollars, so it must be important to somebody in some other way."

I was more than a little surprised at how my praise had rolled off him. "Too bad we don't have Max Gerter here. I wonder how he'd fit these clues together."

"If it were a Gantry plot, we'd have more clues. There's only the one, really."

"Max could do a lot with one clue. That sharp German mind."

"Will you lay off the with the Max Gerter," he said impatiently. "This is serious, Audrey. It must have something to do with Rosalie's death, don't you think? As soon as she died, somebody came running after you and stole that picture. None of her Supreme Court judges or presidential candidates would do that."

"Nobody would. It doesn't make any sense."

"There's Lorraine Taylor, and her daughter," he said pensively.

"Why would they want it? They probably have a lot of Rosalie's other works."

"Did you know Drew runs an art gallery in New York?"

"Rosalie never mentioned it. How do you happen to know that?"

"Don't you do *any* research, Audrey? I read it in the *National Enquirer*."

"The *National Enquirer*! Oh well, in that case there's no possibility of a doubt. I mean, the *National Enquirer* and the Bible. Do you mean to say you, a college professor, actually read the *Enquirer*?"

He had the decency to blush at least. "I read everything. Nothing conceived by human mind is alien to me. I saw Rosalie's picture plastered all over it at the supermarket, and picked one up. It talked about Lorraine and her daughter, who runs a gallery in New York. Drew's gallery is in the phone book, so the *Enquirer* got that right. So," he continued, "to return to my point . . ."

"Just what *is* your point?"

"That Drew Taylor's connected with the theft of your picture, in some way that I haven't been able to figure out yet. It didn't say in the *Enquirer* that Drew inherits anything. Actually Rosalie didn't leave much, considering how much she earned. Her estate only amounted to a couple of hundred thousand."

"But there's Hartland. It's worth a lot. Since Rosalie's dead, I can tell about the daughter now. There won't be any sequel—that was the only reason she wouldn't tell me earlier."

Brad pokered up. "It's more likely the child she wanted to protect than herself. We don't know what Drew's circumstances are. She might be a highly respectable woman, who wouldn't want the world to know she's illegitimate. For that matter, the father could be some guy you and your publisher wouldn't care to tangle with. Besides, you don't even know whether it's true. You'd be laying yourself open to a libel charge if it isn't."

"It's true all right. She said in her diary she was gaining weight, and a letter from a friend hinted at morning sickness. Then later she comes home with a baby—Lorraine does, I mean. Brad, I've been meaning to ask you for ages. Why did you slice those pages out of Rosalie's diary—the ones about her gaining weight?"

Caught off guard, he looked as guilty as sin. Furthermore, his inventive mind failed to throw up any plausible explanation. "I had to. I just had to. Don't ask."

"We'll make a deal. I'll promise not to ask, if you'll promise to tell me."

"You must work for a union." He rubbed his furrowed brow, bending his head so I couldn't read his eyes. When he looked up, I knew he had concocted some improbable answer. "Well," he admitted with a sheepish smile, "you won't like it."

"Try me."

He took my hands and blasted me with his most ravishing, professional smile. "Remember the garbage dump, Audrey? I did it for you." But it wasn't his real, post–garbage dump smile he was wearing. It was the Styrofoam one that accompanied his defrosted gourmet dinners.

"And you razored the pages out of the diary for *you*. Why?"

"Because the magazine I'm doing that article for insisted I have some evidence to substantiate my claim that Rosalie had a child. I don't finger Drew as the offspring. I just say I think she had a child. And even for that, they insisted I have something in black and white."

I had forgotten about the magazine article. "You phoney! Warning *me* not to use it! You just wanted to scoop me."

"No! I'm not saying who the kid is, or even hinting. And at the time I took it, you weren't going to mention your suspicions that Rosalie had a child at all."

"It was a crummy thing to do, and you know it!"

"I *do* know it, and I'm sorry, Audrey. I'm not going to use it, if that helps any."

I proved susceptible to his steaming coffee eyes, and even more so to my memories of the afternoon. What he wasn't saying—but it didn't take a Max Gerter to figure it out—was that he cared enough for me that he was foregoing his stolen scoop.

"Promise you won't use it?"

"Cross my heart and hope to die."

"Okay, I forgive you, but I need those pages back. Then you really are writing an article about Rosalie? How do you find time?"

"I have a whole summer free."

"Unh-unh, Madison. You have to hustle along the next Max Gerter detective book. You might as well confess, Brad. I figured it out. The spaghetti Caruso, the hero an ex-professor. But why did you make him of German ancestry?"

His face looked perfectly blank. "What are you talking about?" he asked, with a genuine frown wrinkling his brow.

"You are Madison Gantry, aren't you?"

"Lord, no. Where'd you get that idea?"

"The letter from Belton, the box of books in your trunk. Who are you, then, if you're not Hume Mason, and you're not Madison Gantry?"

Just when I had begun to doubt it, he owned up sheepishly that he was Madison Gantry. "But I don't tell anybody. I don't do any PR—not even my picture on the cover."

"Why not?"

"I like my privacy."

"I think you're ashamed of it. You think your colleagues at college would put you down. I really liked the book, Brad."

"Well, thanks. I'm glad you did, and now that we've got *that* settled, can we get back to the real case? We need some tangible evidence that links Drew Taylor to the theft."

"Fingerprints? No, it wasn't Drew. She was at the funeral." I slid a leery look at Brad. Had it been he at the funeral? I only got a glimpse. I must have been mistaken.

"She wouldn't do it herself. She'd hire a couple of thugs. There are guys that'll do it for a C note, as Max Gerter would say. The trouble is, that typewriter's been handled more than a public pay phone. There are your prints and mine, the wino's, and the cop's."

"True, and since I don't believe in dusting or housecleaning, there'd be prints from the salesman and everybody else who ever touched it."

"You're the one who said it. Anyway, pros use gloves."

"I could phone Drew," I suggested, though what I would say hadn't occurred to me yet.

"That would alert her you're suspicious."

"All right, what do you suggest then?"

"I suggest we exercise the little gray cells," he said, tapping his temple. "Like Hercule Poirot. I don't waste all my time on Gantry. I also waste it on Agatha Christie. Exercise increases the oxygen supply to the brain. Don't faint—I'm not going to suggest we do jogging. There's a dance floor out there."

"There's a nice hot cup of coffee here," I pointed out.

"Bitter stuff. They use too much cheap Brazilian coffee. Dancing is much better for you. Besides," he added with a glowing smile, "if I don't find some excuse to get my arms around you very soon, I'm going to burst a blood vessel. Your jacket falls open when you reach forward."

I leaned low across the table. "The creamy whites are heaving, are they?"

He took a long look, with eyes that seemed hypnotized. "I can see your heart throb." I could actually feel it throb faster from the concentration of his gaze. "Now they're heaving," he said, and looked up, smiling.

"My bosoms do not heave. They hardly flow. Furthermore, they're not white. I'm getting a tan."

"You knew it was you I was writing about, huh? They were white the last peek I got, when you had on your bathing suit. I'll look into it more closely, and change the manuscript to read 'freckled,' if required. Polka dot nudes are in style this season."

"You're seriously weird, Brad," I decided, and stood up.

"I'll just walk a step behind you like the Duke of Edinburgh, and watch you undulate," he whispered in my ear, as he drew my chair back.

"Voyeur!" His hand settled on my hip. I could feel the

heat of his fingers as we walked, with my hips moving intimately against them.

Only three couples occupied the tiny dance floor. Others sat at tables around the edge, drinking. A combo played soft, romantic music. It was a black-velvet night, the sky sprinkled with stardust, and the reflection of a fat, wan moon danced in the dark water beyond.

A brisk breeze blew in from the river. "Do you think it's going to be warm enough to dance outside?" I asked.

"I feel like a nuclear reactor, ready to melt down. Are you feeling cold?"

"No, I'm fine."

His head bent above mine, *above* being the operative word here. He was tall enough that my head just fit the crook of his shoulder. "Romantic," I sighed. "You'll give me a chance to run for cover if the meltdown starts, won't you? I wouldn't want to glow in the dark."

"Why not? A body like yours should be visible at all times." His arms tightened till our hips clung together as we moved in time to a sinuous Latin rhythm. I felt his lips brush my ear. "If it weren't so corny, I'd say this night was made for love."

"When did corniness ever stop you? Max Gerter actually said he wanted Sophia so bad it hurt."

"I know how he felt."

"Were those creamy bosoms really mine?"

"A man needs inspiration for that kind of purple prose. It doesn't just come from nowhere."

"It was supposed to come from Rosalie's movies. That's what you were writing about."

"Poetic license. I take my inspiration where I find it."

"It's funny, you looked blank when I first asked you if you were Madison Gantry. You're sure you're not Hume Mason?"

"I promise on my mother's grave."

"I bet your mother's alive and well, and living in County Cork, or some dumb Irish place." I smiled dreamily.

"No, she's dead, but I have relatives in County Cork, just a shamrock's throw from Blarney Castle. I've caressed the stone many times. And you know what they say about us stone-kissing, silver-tongued Irishmen."

"Something about having 'a cajoling tongue and the art of flattery . . .' I forget the rest."

"It goes 'or of telling lies with unblushing effrontery.' Straight from *Lewis's Dictionary of Ireland*."

"I never heard of it. I got it from the *Oxford Companion*. Why should I believe a card-carrying, stone-kissing liar?"

"We're getting deep into metaphysics here. Do you believe a liar when he tells you he's lying?"

"I don't do methaphysics after a double martini and half a bottle of wine."

He lifted his head and smiled down at me. "What *do* you do when you're feeling giddy, Audrey?"

"I drink coffee and sober up."

"Daredevil! I have a suggestion to make while you're still tipsy."

A twinge of suspicion tweaked at me. "Is it decent?"

"It's legal, between consenting adults."

My bones firmed up, then stiffened. Finally I came to a halt in the middle of the dance floor. "You know it's getting late, and I have to be up early tomorrow."

"I'll speak to the desk clerk."

He had misunderstood. They say people see what they want to see, and in this case, Brad had heard what he wanted to hear. He thought I was urging him to rush out and reserve a room.

"That won't be necessary. I meant I'd like to go home now." I stalked back to the table. Brad followed behind,

trying not to look foolish. I would not be bulldozed into
going to bed with him or anyone else before I was good and
ready. I began gathering up my cigarettes and lighter and
stuffing them into my purse.

Brad watched me, then said, "Can't we discuss this like
a couple of adults? I'm not talking about a one-night stand.
I take our relationship seriously, Audrey."

"I have been seriously taken, Brad, not taken seriously.
There's a difference. Unfortunately, only one of us is a
grown-up. The other appears to be a sex-starved adoles-
cent."

"It's only natural when a man and woman are together a
lot. I admire you, very much. I like you, and I want you.
What's wrong with that?"

Admiring and liking were fine, in their way. The word
love, however, was conspicuous by its absence. "There's
nothing wrong with it. And there's nothing wrong with my
refusing either. Let's just leave it at that."

"You said when we were better acquainted. We're pretty
well acquainted now, wouldn't you say? Or was that just an
excuse?"

"I don't need an excuse! I don't *owe* you anything. I
didn't ask you to go climbing up the garbage piles—it was
your own idea. I'm leaving now." I strode angrily from the
room.

I went to the parking lot, but his car was locked, so I had
to stand and wait while he paid the bill, which I was
supposed to pay. I'd reimburse him, and give him the ten
bucks he'd paid the wino, too. It was a good ten minutes
before he sauntered out, trying to look nonchalant, with one
hand in his pocket. We didn't exchange a word as he
unlocked the car and got in. He opened my door from the
inside and I let myself in. His pop-up manners were
reserved for more accommodating dates.

He inserted the key, turned it, and a rough, grinding sound resonated in the car. My temper improved slightly to see he wasn't as cool as he pretended. He'd flooded the engine. He tried again, and the grinding turned to a coughing chug.

"Better wait till you and the engine simmer down," I suggested.

He turned the key again immediately, stomping on the gas pedal all the time. This time there was no sound but a light clinking, as of expanded metal parts shrinking. Without a word, Brad got out, lifted the hood, and looked at the perfectly invisible engine. He soon came to my door and said, "I'll have to call a service station. Do you want to go back inside to wait?"

"I'm fine here, thanks."

He stalked back into the restaurant. The pleasure of his discomfort was mitigated by my own. I lit a cigarette, and before I butted it, he was back.

"They're not open till morning," he announced. "Luckily, they have some empty rooms."

"Looks like you aren't the only one who struck out tonight." I followed him back to the restaurant, my mind alive with plans to get home alone. As I chased him to the steps I called, "I want to pay for our dinner."

"Keep it. You can pay for your own room," he answered, in a perfectly bored voice.

He held the door for me to enter, and led the way to the registration desk. I found myself asking for a room, almost before I had time to think about it.

CHAPTER 10

I wasn't calm enough to realize I'd been rash till the bedroom door was closed behind me. Then I asked myself why I hadn't had the sense to find out about a bus, or a taxi if necessary, to get home. It wouldn't have cost as much as this room. But as I *was* registered, with my credit card number already on record, I looked around to see where I'd be spending a sleepless night.

The room was small and cute, in the cloying way a room in a Walt Disney animated film is cute—chintz curtains, pine furniture with little heart cutouts, Norman Rockwell reproductions on the wall. The oversized, satin-draped bed in the corner looked like a lady of pleasure wandered in from a foreign film. I went to the window to draw the drapes, and heard a knock on the door. Brad!

"Who is it?" I called.

"Charles Manson," Brad called. I bit back a reluctant smile and went to the door. "Is everything all right?" he asked.

Since he looked suitably repentant, I decided to let him in. I cast a withering glance around the room and said,

"Couldn't be better. I was just wondering if I wouldn't be in Goldilocks' way."

"You have it all to yourself, Snow White."

"You're confusing your fairy tales."

Brad was holding a newspaper. He handed it to me and said, "I found this in my room. There's a long article about Rosalie in it. Quite a bit of trivial detail about her movies—I thought you might like to see it."

"Thanks." I accepted his peace offering. It was much too early to go to bed, and I wouldn't be able to sleep in a strange place anyway. Brad and I exchanged an uncertain look.

"I'm sorry," he said.

I shrugged magnanimously. "Cars break down."

"I mean about my untimely suggestion. I'll pay for your room, of course."

"Forget it. Oh, and I want to pay you for the dinner."

I went for my purse. Brad took it from my hand and threw it on the bed. "I'm paying for my own room at least," I insisted.

"We'll make a deal. You can pay for your room if you let me stay awhile and keep you company."

I gave him a long, head-shaking look. "You're shameless, you know that. Sit down if you want to, but sit on your hands."

"It's my tongue that should be manacled. Please don't ask why I suggested it. I don't even know. Force of habit, I guess. Yes, it *is* a revealing statement," he continued, apparently reading my mind. "And not true either."

"Lying can become a habit. Let's just forget it."

"I felt I should say something about it. It was a mistake."

"A tactical error," I modified, and pulled out the desk chair to sit down.

"Well, everybody does it. It's permitted nowadays."

"It isn't compulsory. You make a thing permissible, and next year it's a duty. If they made euthanasia legal, every soul over seventy would feel guilty for not eliminating himself. I refuse to feel guilty for not consenting."

Brad sat on the edge of the bed and took out his cigarettes. "My room has a sofa," he mentioned. "If you want to watch TV or something . . ."

My chair was hard, and it would be easier to bolt from his room, should the need arise, than to expel him from mine. "Okay."

We went to his room, which was a larger version of mine, with a mini sitting room at the end of it. "The brochure calls it colonial decor," he explained, looking around. "It's sweet enough to give you a cavity if you stayed longer than twenty-four hours."

"I was just wondering how anyone, even the most confirmed lecher, could choose a place like this to . . ."

"Maybe they turn the lights out. All rooms are black in the dark. Shall I order some beer?"

"Sure, why not."

I fiddled with the TV while he made the call. It was reruns, but by the time the beer came, the news was on and we settled in to listen.

"Do you get a feeling of déjà vu watching this?" I asked. "For as long as I can remember, I've been watching people starve and be shot."

"Turn it off if you want," he suggested. "The trouble with TV is, it trivializes everything. Wars, famine, love . . ." He slid a wary eye my way. I controlled my smile, as I was curious to see how he was going to make an ass of himself this time. "We're all consumers. Things— and people too—are here to be used. Fast cars to be driven, Coke to be drunk, and beautiful women to be . . ."

"That's ingenious, Brad. A lousy excuse isn't necessarily better than none."

He looked offended. "I'm looking for the *reason*, not an excuse. I knew you weren't like a lot of the other women I meet. I didn't want to look like an idiot in front of you. But when you agreed to come here . . ."

"Strangely enough, I thought a dinner invitation meant dinner. It's Pavlov you should be blaming. A motel, a woman—bingo, sex."

"I'm salivating already. But I'm glad you're—different."

"More adult," I reminded him.

" 'Better,' I was going to say."

"Try 'smarter.' I recognize the introduction of a new line."

"Why are you so suspicious?" he demanded. "I'm trying to be nice, to apologize and flatter—*compliment* you."

"With unblushing effrontery! You're trying to get me into bed, Brad, and I wouldn't go now if I wanted to."

"For your information, Audrey, I'm no longer in the mood. I wouldn't go if you begged me."

"So there," I added for him. After a brief silence, I said, "I might as well go back to my own room."

"You might as well if you only came here in the hope of being seduced." I tightened my muscles to flounce up and out, till I saw the laughter in his eyes. "Relax, Audrey. I'm not after your bod—tonight. The appendage can take only so much verbal abuse, then it goes on strike. It's becoming conditioned to retire into quiescence at the very sound of your voice."

"A wise appendage."

"A little sensitive to abuse, like me."

"I was sure you'd both be used to it by now."

"Let's go for a walk," he said, tacitly admitting defeat. We walked down to the river and sat on a bench, looking across the water. A large ghostly galleon of a ship drifted by out in the channel, dodging a few of the thousand islands that dotted the expanse of black water. To the west, the lights of the Thousand Island Bridge to Canada formed a necklace around the river's throat. Overhead, the moon looked distant, white, and eerie. It was pretty enough to melt an iceberg, or a cold woman. We should have come here first and let things develop more naturally. Here I sat by the romantic river with a beautiful hunk of a man who was honor-bound, if he had any honor, not to molest me.

"Kind of like being at a golf course with no balls," he said, looking hopefully at me. "*Golf* balls, I mean," he added hastily, when my lips stirred.

"And a quiescent club," I smiled.

"That's what *you* think. Would you mind very much if I kissed you?"

"What, sully these virginal lips?" I looped my arms around his neck.

With a sigh of infinite satisfaction, he pulled me into his arms and kissed me. It was a very accomplished kiss, warm and satisfying and stirring springlike sensations of awakening as he nibbled my lips apart and invaded with his tongue. I liked the close, bearish feel of his arms protecting me from the cool breeze. Knowing that he wanted more than a kiss lent an edge to things, too.

"We should have come here first," I said, running my fingers over his neck. A neck was such a vulnerable thing, soft and warm.

He took my other hand and held it against his mouth, kissing it. "I'm not really a lech, Audrey. If you don't come on to most women today, they think you're gay. It puts a strain on a guy, you know. Damned if you don't, and once in a rare and wonderful while, damned if you do."

"I hope you don't get the idea I'm frigid or something.

When a man comes on so strong, taking for granted you can't wait to admire his etchings, it gets my back up."

"Don't apologize. I acted like a jerk."

"Jerks are more persistent. They don't warm up such delicious frozen dinners either. Did you really cook them yourself, back home?"

"In a manner of speaking, I did. Pierre was with me, but I did half the work. I don't want you to think I was just interested in your body, Audrey. I like being with you, talking with you, if you can call what we do talking. I think we'd make a fairly decent team."

I looked him in the eye, trying to read, if possible, what the word "team" denoted to him. "Me such a great cook, and you with your insatiable appetite—for food, I mean." He smiled.

"I never eat anything else but."

We kissed again, and again. For a long time we sat on the bench, smooching like high school kids, each waiting for the other to suggest the next step, each too stubborn to be the one to give in. I was curious to see if he'd try to get into my room when we went back inside, and didn't know whether I was glad or sorry that he didn't even try; but I knew I was surprised. His mischievous smile told me he knew it, too.

I slept fairly well in a strange bed, but woke early in the morning. Since it was too early to get up, I just lay there and thought about Brad. He could be charming when he wasn't trying to make out. I thought he could be charming when he succeeded, too. If he hadn't tried so hard, he would have succeeded before now. A man should be told a thing like that—in a discreet way, of course.

I was up, showered, dressed, and considering going to the dining room alone when the tap came at my door.

"Good morning." Brad smiled. "It's a beautiful day out

there. It's too bad you have to work, but I guess you want to get back to your book."

"I have to, want it or not."

"What do you want for breakfast?"

"Bacon and eggs'll be fine."

"Good. I doubt if they have any apples and rye bread." He looked as if he might kiss me before we left, but he didn't.

There was a different waitress in the dining room in the morning. The new one's name was Georgie. She didn't look like a Georgie—more like a Bo or a Loni. She knew Brad by name too, and talked when she brought our food.

"Did you find that Simcoe cottage you were looking for last time you were here, Mr. O'Malley?"

"Yes, I also rented it."

"I don't know why you didn't stay here. Are the Simcoe cottages nice?"

"Not particularly," he said, with feeling.

"Mr. Abrams has rented all his places now. The last one went yesterday. What was the big attraction down the river, that you decided against Abrams' cottage?" she asked.

He gave a quick, self-conscious look at me, and I perked up my ears for his answer. "The fishing's good down that way," he said briefly.

"We have the best fishing in this part of the river," Georgie objected. "A guy caught a twenty-pound muskie yesterday. You didn't mention anything about fishing."

"Would you please get me some—ketchup," he said quickly.

Georgie wriggled off. "Ketchup—something new for the gobbling gourmet," I mentioned. "What *was* the big attraction at Simcoe's place, Brad?"

"It's a bit busy here, with the boat tours and tennis. I

wanted privacy." He poured cream in his coffee and looked around the restaurant, trying for an air of ease.

A boat tour took people away, and the tennis courts were hardly enough attraction to inundate the place with tourists. If he'd wanted total isolation, he wouldn't have been banging at my door every half hour. Simcoe's place was a dump, while the cottages here were charming, in their own Walt Disney way.

My icy stare was waiting for him when he finished looking around the restaurant. "You went to Simcoe's place because you knew *I* was there," I said firmly, not allowing any hint of a question to mar it.

"I didn't know you were there till after I moved in."

"I think you did. I'm not suggesting it was my charms that lured you hither. It was my research, and you *are* Hume Mason!"

"Don't be ridiculous! I told you I wasn't." He tried to take refuge in anger, but his heart wasn't in it. Guilt made him soft.

Georgie came back and banged the ketchup bottle on the table. As soon as she left, I resumed my attack. "Why were you asking around for Simcoe's place, if not to find me? It's not famous, certainly not the kind of a place a would-be jet-setter like you would seek out for its prestige, so why?"

When he didn't defend himself against the jet-set charge, I knew I was right. "I heard about it," he said vaguely.

"How? Did Belton put a sleuth on my tail when they heard I was doing the book? You had easy work getting at my research. I want you to know, I think you're a contemptible phoney. I won't be going back with you, and I don't suggest you break into my cottage and steal my box again. Or did you have it photocopied?"

He ignored my question. "Look who's talking about

breaking into cottages! You rifled my drawers, and read my manuscript."

"Yes, *manuscript*! I knew it wasn't anything else but. If that manuscript is a sample of the hatchet job you're doing on Rosalie, I hope her daughter sues you! And furthermore, I want those two pages you cut out of the diary returned in good condition." I pushed away my plate to remove the temptation of dumping it on his head.

He pushed it back at me and said, "I told you, I'm not Hume Mason."

"Fine, let's go out and open that carton of paperbacks you carefully locked in the trunk of your car, shall we?"

"I'm eating my breakfast now," he said, with an effort at calm loftiness.

It was too much to bear. "Since you're so hungry, eat mine too." I lifted my plate and took aim. I regret to this day that he ducked, and I only caught his shoulder, but even that aroused some interest in the other breakfasters.

The only thing left to do after that was to stride angrily from the dining room, not stopping till I reached the reception desk. I enquired for bus service east, and learned there was none. The clerk told me if I walked about three miles to the highway, there'd be a bus at ten after twelve. My sandals weren't made for walking.

"After twelve? I've got to get away immediately."

"Your best bet'd be a taxi," he decided, after much rubbing of whiskers. "Orbison's taxi will be operating in a couple of hours. He doesn't bother running it till ten. The best business is at night. He works late, and starts at ten in the morning."

"That's too late. Is there a car rental?"

"Nope." He smiled complacently. "You'd have to take the taxi into Alexandria Bay for that. There'll be a bus in—"

"Is there *any* way out of here, other than walking or swimming?"

"Well now," he said, stroking his jaw, "I just might be able to help you. Going east, you say?"

"Yes."

"Wait here."

He ambled off and came back in five minutes to tell me there was a customer driving east in a few minutes. He'd be happy to take me with him. He'd be a noisy traveling salesman—if I was lucky—but at that point I hardly cared if he was a mass murderer.

"Thank you." He looked expectant, so I gave him five dollars. I felt like demanding it back when it was Brad who came sauntering to the counter ten minutes later. His shoulder was wet where he'd washed the egg yolk and bacon grease from it.

He wore a jeering smile. "Ready to leave? You might as well have eaten breakfast. It wasn't half-bad. You should always make sure, before a grand exit, that there's not an anticlimax waiting in the wings to humiliate you." His smile stretched to a grin.

"Like a car with a broken engine, you mean?" I retaliated.

"It turns out I just flooded the engine. I tried it this morning and it was fine."

"You did it on purpose, you creep! You're pathetic, you know that? A man your age acting like a raunchy teenager. I'm surprised you didn't run out of gas."

His nostrils dilated. "*My* age? I'm not quite senile yet." I saw the age arrow had hit home.

"Not quite." I smiled, staring at his wrinkles.

He stomped out; I hurried after him. No matter how degrading to my ego, I wasn't going to let Hume Mason get back to work hours before me.

At the car, he stopped, eyes narrowed, and said, "Are you sure you want to share a ride with a pathetic old creep?"

"I'll have myself fumigated when I get home."

I sat with my arms crossed, glaring out the window till we reached the cottage. Not another word passed between us, even when he exceeded the speed limit by several miles an hour in an effort to jolt my mouth open. When he parked under the tree, I opened my own door and strode to my cottage. I didn't say good-bye or thank you, or even look over my shoulder. I rather thought he'd be childish enough to say "You're welcome," but he didn't say it.

I went straight to my typewriter, though I didn't intend to work in my best suit. When my seething anger simmered down, I realized I was in no condition even to type, let alone compose anything. My fingers were shaking. He'd done it again. Gotten me so upset I couldn't work. I had a feeling the typewriter keys next door were already clattering out seventy or eighty words a minute.

CHAPTER 11

Every time I had anything to do with Brad O'Malley, I ended up looking like a dope. One melting smile and I'd handed over the diaries. It was no less than a breach of trust for me to have spilled Rosalie's beans. To have spilled them into Hume Mason's dish to be turned into a sleazy travesty was not only stupid but unprofessional. And when I at last had my research back, did I get on with the job? No, I went gallivantaing off to celebrate, and wasted a whole night and half a morning because that wretch convinced me his car had broken down.

Even now, I sat wallowing in self-pity and remorse instead of getting on with the job. I sharpened pencils, arranged paper—all the make-work tricks to stave off the actual writing. Eventually I settled down to read over the last written bit of manuscript, centered a page in the machine, and looked to see the film ribbon was in place. I looked, without really thinking, at a series of numbers. It was a minute before I realized they shouldn't have been there. I hadn't been typing numbers; I'd been typing words.

The ribbon popped out by applying pressure on a lever at the side of the machine. I pulled another inch of ribbon

loose and saw the words *New York, N.Y.*, then the numbers.
My curiosity mounted higher. I pulled some more, and read
Drew Taylor's name and address. It was an apartment on
the East Side, not her gallery. When I pulled the cartridge
apart I found that it was the only message not typed by me.
Therefore it had been surely typed by whoever stole my
machine, my research, my painting.

In my excitement, I forgot all about Brad O'Malley; but
when there was a knock at the door, I figured it had to be he,
so I stuffed the ribbon cartridge under a stack of papers. I
don't even know why I did it, except that I didn't want to
share anything more with him. But it was Simcoe at the
door.

"Hello, Miss Dane. I see you and young O'Malley got
back all right. Have a nice holiday?" His eyes glittered with
curiosity.

"Very nice, thank you." I hoped my tone discouraged
meaningless conversation.

"Next time you go away overnight, you should let me
know. I don't like to think of the cottages being empty, after
the break-in. You took the fiancé home to meet your folks,
I suppose?" he asked, fishing for news.

To satisfy him, I said, "Yes."

"It's real romantic, having lovebirds in our cottages. I
guess you were pretty surprised to find O'Malley land in on
you, eh? I knew he was coming half a day before, but let
him have his little surprise. He asked me not to tell you he
was coming."

I had proof positive that he'd followed me here, and there
could be no conceivable reason other than my research. "He
likes surprises," I said inanely. "The funny thing is I didn't
even give him the address. I wonder how he found the
place."

"He knew the general area you were coming to. He drove

around till they gave him my phone number down at the
Bay. He called up and asked if Miss Dane had hired a
cottage. When I said you had, he snapped up the other quick
as blinking, and told me not to tell you he was coming. He
wanted to surprise his fiancée. He didn't even come to look
at the place first."

"He surprised me all right," I admitted.

"I'll let you get back to work. Remember, if you go off
again, just give me a call, and I'll keep an eye on things for
you."

"Thanks, Mr. Simcoe."

I closed the door and leaned against it, chewing over this
new piece of duplicity on Brad's part. I was so mad I forgot
the typewriter ribbon with Drew's name and address on it.
How was anybody supposed to work in such an atmosphere? I retrieved the ribbon and checked to see I hadn't
imagined the message on it.

It was still there. And last night Brad had led me by the
nose to connect Drew Taylor with the theft from my
cottage. But *he* was the thief—wasn't he? Except it was
peculiar that he helped me get my research back. He said he
didn't know Drew. Furthermore, I didn't think he'd be
careless enough to leave the ribbon with Drew's name in the
machine if he had typed it. He was up on his detective lore
from those Madison Gantry books he read (or possibly
wrote?). But if he was Madison Gantry, why did he refuse
to open the cardboard carton from Belton in the trunk of his
car? The typing of Drew's name and address looked as if it
had been done by an amateur typist. The spacing between
words was wrong, and one of the capitals omitted.

When there was another knock on the door, I went with
rising temper to get rid of Simcoe. I opened the door to see
Brad standing there with a bouquet of wildflowers held
toward me.

"If you're looking for a funeral, you've come to the wrong place. If you care to stick around, however . . ."

He wore the abject frown of a scolded boy. "I come in peace," he answered, but his raised hand showed he was ready to defend himself, if not attack. He proffered the flowers again; I ignored them.

"Fine, you can go back the same way." I tried to close the door, but his toe held it ajar. He was wearing his sandals, which left his toes vulnerable to attack. I pushed harder; his fingers wrapped around the door edge and he pushed it open, squeezing in like a vacuum-cleaner sales-man.

"You can throw those weeds out. I get hay fever." I examined him with the greatest curiosity. It should have taken him longer than this to recover after I'd thrown my breakfast on his shirt.

"Weeds?" he objected, deeply offended. "These are lilies of the valley, denoting a return of happiness in the language of flowers. A lovely thought, don't you think? Buttercups, clover, mock orange, purloined at risk to life and limb from the missus's bush, right under her nose, with the curtain jiggling. A branch of lilac for the scent," he added, pulling out the blossom and handing it to me.

I wasn't totally immune to the spectacle of a handsome man making a jackass of himself over me. Some traitorous corner of my heart wanted to hear an explanation that would exonerate him, but I was mad at myself for the weakness.

"Cut the bullroar," I said. "Simcoe just let the cat out of the bag—about your surprise for the little fiancé.e."

His jaw muscles tensed in frustration. "Blew the whole thing, huh? Audrey, I came to apologize, and to make a deal. If you own a Bible, bring it on. If not, the *Oxford English Dictionary* will do. Whatever my reason for coming here, I want to promise I'm not going to do a book on

Rosalie Hart. I'll take an oath on it." His voice had the ring of truth.

"Will you put it in writing?"

"I'll write it in blood, if you like."

"I'll get a knife." His eyes flew open wider, but even this threat didn't deter him. "You admit you *did* come here to share my research?"

"I had it in mind, I confess. I didn't know you then, Audrey. I'm sorry as hell. You mean more to me than any book. Even the *Oxford Dictionary*," he said rashly. "More than *Bartlett's Familiar Quotations*. What else can I say?"

I felt a smile moving my lips. "More than Eliot?"

"Sweetheart, more than Eliot and Shakespeare combined." He smiled disarmingly. "Are we friends?" he asked, once more shoving the bouquet at me.

"I suppose." I took the weeds and put them in one of the peanut butter glasses beside my typewriter. I wanted to go on being angry with him, but my heart was melting for relief and joy. I remembered the cartridge ribbon, and pulled it out to show him what I'd found.

"Why did you type this when you stole my typewriter?" I inquired. He frowned in perplexity. "You might as well admit the whole thing now, while I'm in a forgiving mood. You took my stuff, didn't you?"

"I *didn't*! That's what's driving me crazy. And that's why I don't think it was your research that was the point of the whole thing. What's written on that?"

I handed him the ribbon and he read the last bit. "Drew Taylor!" he exclaimed, eyes alight. "There's our hard evidence linking her to your polka dot nude. You see, you wronged me, thinking *I'd* stolen your stuff. It all had to do with Drew Taylor and the painting."

"I still don't see why she'd do such a thing."

"Why don't you ask her?" he suggested simply.

"You said I shouldn't phone her—it would tip her off that we know something. Though I'm not quite sure just what it is we know."

"There's just the name and address on the ribbon. What does that suggest to you?"

"An envelope, I guess, but why wouldn't her henchman just phone her? It's faster."

"Right, and it doesn't leave any evidence, so it likely wasn't an envelope. And if it wasn't an envelope, it must have been a label, to put on a package," he announced, with a triumphant smile.

"Are you sure you're not Madison Gantry?" He hunched his shoulders. "The package contained my painting, you mean?"

"Right on. You're going to say why not just take the picture to her."

"Consider it said."

"I will. Now, let's run over the scenario. You were here in the cottage when the guy—or whoever—broke in. Naturally you'd report the theft as soon as you discovered it."

"That's what I did. So what? The thief was long gone by then."

"It's my guess he went back to wherever he was staying—some local motel probably—and *did* phone Drew. He told her he'd got the picture, and confused the issue by picking up whatever else was handy. He probably intended to hock the machine, maybe back in New York. Drew, being a more clever lady, tells him to dump everything else, and send her the picture in the mail. That way, if he gets picked up, the picture is safe. *He's* safe too—there's no evidence on him. And Simcoe got a look at the car earlier on, remember. I'm assuming your Peeping Tom was the thief, so there was some danger the car could be identified.

He had the typewriter in his motel room, trying to decide what he could get for it. He'd have to go out and buy paper and tape and labels, when Drew ordered him to mail the picture. He plugs in the typewriter and types the label, then dumps it and the rest of the stuff at the incinerator and gets back to New York fast. You can see by the ribbon the typing was done by an amateur. I am *not* an amateur, Audrey."

"I'm just wondering why he rented a motel room."

"He'd have to come from New York in daylight to find the cottage. It's not exactly standing on a public road. He needed some place to pass the time till midnight or thereabouts. He'd sack out in a motel."

"I guess he might have done that. But how did Drew know where to find me? Of course she's Rosalie's daughter, and Rosalie and Lorraine Taylor knew," I said, thinking out loud. "I told them the address, in case Rosalie wanted to get in touch with me, so Drew could have found out. It fits."

"Like a bosom in a bra."

"You're a monomaniac."

"A hungry man sees food in ink blots," he explained. "Let's tackle Drew."

"I hardly know what to say to her. Her name on a ribbon isn't much proof. I could have typed it myself."

"It's not hard police evidence. That'll come later. Why don't you leave it up to me?" he suggested. "Since I'm not writing my book, I can spare the time. I always wanted to give this kind of thing a try."

"Are you going to phone, or go to New York in person?"

"In person. I want to see her face when she starts her song and dance. You can tell a lot about a woman from her face. Like yours, for instance, when you wanted to be mad at me when I came in."

"I *was* mad."

"Yes, but you were sorry, too. Real hard, black-and-blue

mad would have got that door closed. It would have thrown my weeds in my face—like you threw your breakfast this morning. *Then* you were mad. You're like me, Audrey. You blow up, and then get over it in a hurry. We're going to have some beautiful blowups together." A proprietory arm was slipping around me.

"Don't press your luck," I advised, with a long, sideways look at him. But I couldn't stop the smile that slowly broke out.

"I always do. At my age, I haven't got a minute to waste." He pulled me close for a lingering, leisurely kiss that blew away any remaining webs of anger and doubt. He had to love me. My body couldn't be that stupid, that it didn't know the difference between love and sex.

When he lifted his head, his eyes were alight with a hopeful gleam. He glanced toward the bedroom and said, "I don't have to leave this very minute."

"Time, as they say, is of the essence."

"Haste makes waste. Seems a shame to waste . . ."

"Can't bear to leave me, huh?" I asked, detaching myself. During the ensuing friendly wrestling match, I accidentally stepped on his toes, rather hard.

"You're mean when you're aroused," he exclaimed, hopping on one foot.

"I'm not aroused to anything but curiosity, at the moment. Brad, I think I'll go with you. I'm too upset to work here, and I don't have to race like a fiend now that you're not doing your book. I can do some thinking and planning while you drive."

"But what about . . ." He looked with yearning eyes to the bedroom door.

I batted my eyes furiously and said, "Heaven can wait."

The sun filtered through leafed trees, tracing patterns on the grass beyond the window. I was mentally justifying and rationalizing my desire to play truant. After all, Drew Taylor was Rosalie's daughter—a part of Rosalie's life. And it was just possible that Brad knew a few details I'd missed too, since he must have done some minimal research.

"The trip wouldn't be a complete waste of time," I said.

"Thank you. It's nice to know my company isn't totally without merit."

"Of course not. You must know a few things about Rosalie that I don't."

His ardor was quickly sinking to annoyance. "You're making me quiescent again, Audrey," he warned.

"Go home and get ready, Brad. I have to change."

"I guess you won't want to travel in your only decent—" I stopped him with a gimlet eye. "Ahem. In your nice white suit," he finished, and left, rather quickly.

That sounded like tacit acknowledgment that he didn't object to being seen with a woman in jeans and a T-shirt. I phoned Simcoe to tell him we were leaving, and put my white suit in a hang-up bag to take along, in case we went out that night. The precious research I put in a clothes closet with blankets on top of it. After I flung a nightie and toilet articles into a hand bag, I locked the front door and went out to his car.

CHAPTER 12

"You're prompt," Brad complimented, when he joined me five minutes later. "I see you've reverted to your Raggedy Ann style."

"I'd rather be comfortable than stylish."

I made myself comfortable in the car while Brad stashed our bags and took over the chore of driving. "What do you suppose Drew's doing with Rosalie's pictures—if she even has them, I mean?" I mused.

"She must have them; they weren't at Hartland."

"Just because I didn't see them doesn't mean they weren't there, in the attic or some place."

"You can take it from me, they weren't there. Gone, vanished, the lot of them," he assured me.

His air of concern certainly revived a former suspicion. "You *were* there! You broke into her house and searched it. Brad, was it when you were at her funeral? You were there too, weren't you, when you told me Sean had fallen out of a tree?" The questions tumbled out in my excitement.

"Where'd you get that idea?"

"You were on TV."

"Damn, I thought I ducked the camera."

"I thought it was you. Since you're not writing your book, maybe you can give me some details for mine. About the funeral, I mean."

He looked uncomfortable with the subject, but obliged me. "There wasn't much of anything unusual. There was a bird in the church. I noticed it soaring high up in the vaulted arch. It was touching, somehow. I pictured it being Rosalie's soul coming to her own funeral. The restless spirit free from its mortal cage at last, to soar into the delirious blue."

I made a disparaging face. "Was the ceiling of the church blue, or did it have a hole in it?"

"You have a very literal, unpoetic soul, Audrey. I saw it as a symbol. A little symbolism doesn't do an opus any harm."

"I'll let Mason deal with the mumbo-jumbo. What kind of a bird was it?" It was a fact that the bird was there after all, and if some deluded reader wanted to make a symbol of it, it was up to him.

"A swallow," he said, and immediately changed the subject. "I bet Lorraine channeled the pictures out to Drew in New York over the years, and Drew sold them. If the paintings Rosalie did in France were all as good as your nude, she might have passed them off as originals. Don't laugh!" he objected, when I snorted in derision. "It would be easier than you think. Most of those artists are dead now. Some of the work was actually done at the artists' own studios, with their materials. Matisse, Léger, Braque, Rouault—she mentioned them all in her diaries."

"She even said that Braque thought her painting of a peasant boy was a Picasso!"

"The experts often spot a forgery by the materials used, but if she worked in their studios, with their canvas and paints . . . Of course that wouldn't apply to all her works—your pointillist one, for instance. Both Pissarro and

Seurat died around the turn of the century, but some of the others might pass examination." He stopped, frowning.

"Rosalie signed the pictures in her own name. At least she signed mine."

"Apparently she didn't sign the one Braque mistook for a Picasso. Not that it would be impossible to change the signature. It's probably that telltale signature that had Drew worried about your painting—or maybe it's the fact that it's posing as a late-1800s piece. The pigments wouldn't match that era. It could be proven a phoney by chemical analysis."

"If she'd done a different imitation, I might still have it," I said wistfully. "Wouldn't you think somebody would have caught on before now, if Drew's been doing this for years?"

"We don't know how long Drew's been running her gallery. That's one thing to find out. She wouldn't risk selling to museums or well-versed collectors if there was something shady about her product. She'd probably try to get them out of the country, or deep in the heart of Texas, someplace out of the mainstream."

"How do you plan to extract all this from Drew? You're obviously not going to tell her who you are."

"Why shucks, ma'am, I reckon I just blew in from Texas in my private jet," he said, in a southern drawl. "Actually," he went on in his own accent, "Texas isn't out of the mainstream of art. All that oil money. We'll snoop around her gallery and see what we can find. Maybe I'll revert to my Irish brogue, become a wealthy Irish horsebreeder, stopping off on my way to Kentucky to pick up a bit of Yankee culture—French paintings—to take home to the ould sod with me." He finished this speech in a very creditable brogue.

"You do that well."

"That's my real tongue. This phoney American accent I

use is becoming second nature now. I wanted to fit in when I came to the States, and worked hard to lose my accent."

"You'd make a good actor, with that facility for dialects."

"I hope so. I'll have some acting to do with Drew Taylor. How'd you like to be my secretary?"

"I don't do accents. I can be your American hostess," I said. I noticed he hadn't suggested we pose as man and wife, and mentioned it, in an oblique way.

"Drew's a swinging single," he told me. "She likes men. I observed her, discreetly, at the funeral. There's no danger she'd recognized me. She didn't even see me, with all the movie stars and moguls around."

It was a long trip, between six and seven hours, but through pretty countryside, with a stop for lunch along the way. It was four-thirty when we found Drew's gallery and a place to park. Having seen the glamorous—and beautiful—Drew Taylor on TV at Rosalie's funeral, I wanted to change and freshen up before going to the gallery, but there wasn't time for it.

We learned one important fact before we entered the door. The gold lettering on the black building front gave the opening date as three years ago. "Interesting, Ms. Andrews," Brad said, nodding at it. "She's a relative newcomer in the business."

"Is that my name—Andrews?"

"Vivian Andrews."

"I don't like Vivian. Make it Annabelle, or Charlene."

"We want an invisible name. I'll call you Ms. Andrews. And you can tell me Mr. O'Casey."

"Faith and bejaebbers, I thought Sean was your son, not your da."

"You're right—you don't do accents. You're from Kentucky. You met me here in New York, and are going to accompany me to your famous brood farm in Kentucky."

"What I don't know about horses would fill a library."

"I'll do the talking, and I hope Drew's as ignorant as you."

We walked into the gallery, where half a dozen original oil paintings, none of them by famous names, were propped on easels around the walls of the room. There was no salesperson present, but within a minute a beaded curtain rattled and a woman glided forward. She wasn't young, but not yet old either. Somewhere between thirty-five and forty—the right age for Rosalie's daughter. A sleek wave of toffee-colored hair fell over her cheek in careful abandon. She had the arched brow, high cheekbones, and sculptured nose that suggested superior breeding. I felt intimidated even before she opened her mouth. I recognized the apparition as Drew Taylor.

"Can I help you?" she asked, as she directed her dazzling smile to Brad.

"You can," he said, laying on the brogue. "I came looking for some paintings. If yours are as pretty as yourself, I came to the right place." His brown eyes were all over her, and his smile was broad as it was lascivious. "You're the prettiest picture I've seen since my plane landed. I'm O'Casey Castlecomer—the old country. You've heard of the O'Casey stables," he said.

Drew sidestepped the question. "Are you a neighbor of the Aga Khan? I understand he has a stud farm in Ireland."

"Not close neighbors to Ballymany. That's in Kildare County."

"I confess I'm not an afficionada. I'm Drew Taylor, the proprietress here. What sort of pictures are you looking for, Mr. O'Casey? Is it something to do with horses?"

"Horses?" he asked, and laughed. "Ah no, those beauties

can only be appreciated in the flesh. I'm here in America to pick up a mare from this lady's father. The Andrews brood farm, in Kentucky."

"Miss Andrews, delighted," Drew said. She reached to shake my hand, but the light in her topaz eyes was dimmed till she returned her gaze to Brad.

"Aye, we'll breed a race of winners with the mating," Brad continued, laying it on thicker by the minute. "Between our two stables, how many Derby winners is it we've had, Miss Andrews?"

"Three," I hazarded, aiming for an impressive but credible number.

A deep laugh shook the air. "She's a great joker, Miss Taylor. Three! We'd have five out of Castlecomer, going back to my grandpa's days."

My faux pas wasn't much noted. Already Drew had a possessive arm on Brad's sleeve, and was leading him to various easels around the room. Her long painted nails and ringed fingers winked under the lights.

"This is a marvelously talented new artist I'm representing," she said. I looked at a talented pattern of black lines of multicolored smear of pigment.

"It's lively, it is," Brad said, but with little enthusiasm. "To tell the truth, it's something more lifelike I'm looking for. Not so modern, if you know what I mean, but not old and dull either. My father, God rest his soul, had the gallery full of old Flemish things. The women look like witches, everyone of them, though he paid a fine pound for them in the old days. They're worth something handsome now. My own taste is more modern."

"But you don't care for abstract expressionism," Drew said, nodding her head.

"If I can't tell what I'm looking at, I like to be able to make an educated guess at least. On the other hand, I don't want any paintings of soup cans or hamburgers. The female figure is what I prefer," he added bluntly. "God's own finest creation, and if it's an undraped figure, I have no objection at all to that."

Drew gave a very knowing smile. "I understand, Mr. O'Casey."

Brad placed a hand on her forearm and said, "Why don't you call me Timothy. You know what I'm after now. Renoir, for instance, I call a painter." His fingers tightened on her arm. She turned and slanted an encouraging smile up at him from the corner of her eye.

"But he generally left the clothes on," she pointed out.

His eyes mentally stripped Drew of her clothes. "Too often," he agreed sadly. "Modigliani would take them off, but he's got a hard edge to him I don't agree with. The old boys now, Reubens and company, they understood how to paint a woman. His colors were well done, soft and hazy, like the Impressionists."

We made a cursory tour of the shop, then we were ushered through the beaded curtain to view other paintings. I saw Brad's head swivelling around, like my own, to see if my nude was amongst them. None of the names represented was famous enough to bother forging. There were no works by Rosalie's friends. Brad took a quick look around and said, "Thank you kindly. I was just passing by and dropped in. I'll walk along to the next place. Maybe you could recommend a reputable gallery to me? I don't collect cheap paintings. I want a name that will hold up, an established name, but I want a picture that will give me pleasure too. It's the taxes that kill us, you know. You've got to invest in something, and buying land hobbles you with taxes and poachers and tenants that don't pay their rent."

"So wise of you." She smiled. "You'll be taking your painting back to Ireland with you, Mr. O'Casey?"

"Timothy!" he reminded her, shaking a playful finger. "I will, yes. I'll take it right home with me. Folks think there's no art in Ireland, only because they never get a chance to see it. I can tell you, Lord Falkenburg has a dandy collection, and two or three others right there in Leinster close to home have got two dozen masterpieces between them. Nothing to match my family's collection, of course," he added proudly.

Drew listened closely, then spoke. "I happen to have a few modern paintings in my own private collection," she said hesitantly. "They're not really for sale . . ." she added with tantalizing uncertainty.

"Then they'd not be much good to me. Could you name another gallery?" Brad asked.

"I think you'd like them," she continued. "I'm thinking of selling one or two, to make room for a new artist I've begun collecting. A German abstract painter—you wouldn't be interested in him. Why don't you drop around to my apartment this evening, Timothy?" she suggested.

"Was there anything in particular we had to do this evening, Miss Andrews?" he asked me.

"No, nothing."

"That's fine then. If you'll give me your address, I'll stop by this evening."

"I'll give you my card. Say, nine o'clock?" she suggested. She lifted a card from a brass salver on her desk and gave it to Brad. "You'd be paying cash, I take it?"

"A certified check, if that's good enough for you. I only have twenty-five hundred in traveler's checks, but my bank will transfer some funds from home. I set it up before I left, to cover the purchase of the mare."

"That'll be fine." She smiled. "I'll look forward to seeing you. Oh, and good-bye, Miss Anderson," she added as an afterthought.

Drew accompanied us to the door. As we passed beyond view, Brad handed me the card, which held the familiar address.

"I have a distinct feeling Miss Andrews was not included in that invitation to view her etchings. I might as well have been invisible. It must be the jeans."

"Yeah, the lack of a y chromosome. I told you, she likes men."

"She's too old for you, Brad."

He smiled in surprise. "Too old for a pathetic old creep like me?"

"That one really hit home, I see."

"Nothing was said about your coming with me. Come along if you've a mind to."

"You can cut the brogue now," I said irritably. "There wasn't a sign of Rosalie's paintings there. This is going to be a lot trickier than we thought."

"She has them at her apartment."

"How is Mr. Timothy O'Casey going to get a certified check from a bank?"

"By opening an account in his name and depositing money."

"How much do you figure we're talking about?"

"Something in the neighborhood of fifty thou will be her asking price."

"A mere bagatelle. You might be as well take two."

"Do you think people really buy those awful smears she had up on the stands?" he asked. "I could do better than that."

"A blind monkey could do better. If people don't buy them, then she's crooked for sure. I'd like to know her rent for that shop, and the apartment."

We came to a corner and waited for the light. "What do you want to do now?" I asked.

"I planned to take you to Le Pavillon d'Antibes for dinner."

"Your French restaurant! Great! Is it fancy?"

He turned a leary eye on my jeans. "We can go to my place to change."

"You have an apartment in New York?"

"I live in New York."

"I didn't see how you could possibly have time to teach literature, with all those quickie books you do."

"I used to teach. I gave it up when the demand for my books exceeded what I could supply on a part-time basis. Once I gave up the teaching, there was no reason to go on living in a small city, away from the action."

"Where's your apartment? No, let me guess. Sutton Place?" He shook his head. "Park Avenue?"

"Close, but no cigar. Central Park West."

I had already felt out of place in the expensive art gallery. I'd hardly said a word, I was so awed by Drew Taylor. Brad's apartment would be equally intimidating—I knew it before I got into his car. I could almost feel my back arch in preparation of being uncomfortable. My conversation dwindled to monosyllables as we drew near. It disappeared entirely when the doorman bowed ceremoniously and greeted Mr. O'Malley with a touch of his cap. The marble-floored lobby, hung in wheat silk, didn't do anything to revive my conversation. I felt as though I had hay stuck in my hair, to match my jeans and sneakers. Mixed in with my feelings of inadequacy was a burning resentment that Hume Mason's sleazy writing paid so inordinately well. For some reason, Helen came to mind. Helen should be coming home from Greece this week. I'd have to call, and let her brag about the honeymoon.

CHAPTER 13

The apartment was all I feared, and more. We entered into a hushed atmosphere, the only sound the whisper of an air conditioner purring softly. A sweep of brown marble hallway stretched toward the horizon, terminating in a shattered statue of some Greek god, mounted on a big pedestal. I had the uncomfortable feeling of being in someone else's church, not knowing quite what was expected of me. Maybe I should genuflect, or bless myself. I looked uncertainly at Brad, who had gone on to another archway and was waiting for me. He was very much at home, a full-fledged member of this temple to mammon. I waded through a Persian rug, eyes darting hither and thither to admire the room's appointments. Even with one rug and the Barcelona chair missing, the place was fully furnished. Only the apartment's vast dimensions saved it from being overcrowded.

Brad hadn't become a connoisseur of art at the gallery without some preparation. If the long-necked, red-haired beauty with the black ellipses for eyes wasn't a genuine Modigliani, she was a better copy than even Rosalie could do. Modigliani was accompanied by other famous names.

The sun-dappled lake bordered with trees reeked of Monet. Renoir was there, too, along with a saint who belonged in a stained-glass window. A Rouault, definitely. The oldest work in the room wasn't an oil painting, but a sketch. It was of a hare cowering beneath a bush, ready to dart off. I took a liking to the hare immediately, felt akin to it, with its dark simple looks, trapped amidst all the finery. In the lower left corner the date *1508* was printed, with a capital *D* in a little framed box. I knew I was looking at an original Albrecht Dürer. The hair on the back of my neck crept with the sensation of awe. All the pictures wore embossed gilt frames twice as big as the actual painting required.

"What's this, your gilt-edged securities?" I joked, to cover my awe.

"Yeah, how do you like them?"

"Impressive," I said, and looked idly around the rest of the room. I wasn't personally acquainted with the furnishings, but they looked as if they might have names, like the Barcelona chair. "Aren't you going to introduce me to your acquisitions?" My voice was involuntarily beginning to take on its tone of irony used to conceal a rampant sense of jealousy and inferiority.

He looked askance, and ignored the jibe. "Want something to drink?"

"Sure, a beer, if you have one. Don't bother with a glass. The bottle's fine. Is it okay if I sit on this, or is it only for show?" I tossed a negligent nod toward a low-slung sofa in ivory suede. It was gorgeous. I would have killed for that sofa. The window above it overlooked Central Park.

"It can take your weight. Just make yourself comfortable."

"I'll try." A small snort of derision escaped me.

Brad's jaw muscle quivered once before he said, "I'll be right back."

It was hard to be comfortable in this temple. The old insecurities came storming over me, leaving me prey to my devices of sarcasm and put-down. And again I was besieged by the unfairness of Brad's acquiring so much luxury with so little real effort and/or talent.

I no sooner sat on the sofa than I heaved myself up and went to read the little bronze plates beneath the paintings. Genuine. Every one of them. I strolled round the room, lifting the decorative pottery to read the names on the bottoms. Bustelli, Meissen, Se`vres. When I'd determined their names and pedigrees, I went to the Renoir painting. I touched the blobs of impasto, and throbbed with envy.

From the archway, Brad's voice suddenly echoed in the room. "The people who know about these things don't recommend playing with the pictures," he said playfully.

I jumped a foot. He came forward and handed me an open can of beer. "Thanks," I said. "Those so-called books of yours must pay well." Now why had I added that mean "so-called"?

"My so-called books keep me in the style to which I have become accustomed—by the sweat of my own so-called brow."

"You have a very impressive apartment, Brad," I said, and gave a condescending smile.

"You've already paid that compliment. Glad you approve. Would you like a tour?"

"Sure, if you're eager to show it off." I was on thorns to see the rest of it.

"We'll start with the library and office, where I do my so-called writing." I sensed that his patience was wearing thin. He strode angrily down the hall that had the statue at the end, flung open a door, and pushed a light switch.

By swallowing hard I suppressed the gasp that rose up in my throat. It wasn't fair. It just wasn't fair that he had such aids to his damnable, cheap writing. The first room was a library, a long room lined with oak shelves, on which rested five or six thousand books. There were matched sets of everything— *Encyclopedia Britannica, Great Books of the Western World,* the *Unabridged Oxford Dictionary,* and rows of classics. A whole section was devoted to history, which surprised me. There were rows of art books, gourmet cookbooks, books on writing and drama and poetry, all systematically arranged like a public library. I couldn't even accuse him of conspicuous consumption. The books were well thumbed.

"This must save you a lot of trips to the library," I said, determined to be unimpressed.

He had decided to retaliate. "My secretary does the leg work. She's deductible."

"I didn't realize Hume Mason was interested in history. You don't write books about historical figures, do you?"

"Like a lot of English lit majors, I minored in history. My office is in here," he said, and opened a door into a computer room. "This is the one that really sayes time. No retyping once the manuscript is done."

Jealousy escalated to black envy. It was a dream. I remembered urging him to buy an electric typewriter, and his modest answer that he intended to look into it. Laughing at me all the time!

"A pity it didn't fit in the trunk of your car with the Cuisinart; you could have used it for Rosalie's book." I turned to leave immediately. From the corner of my eye, I had an impression of a wall of filing cabinets, another desk with an electric typewriter, and more bookshelves.

"It would have saved me some work, but it wasn't practicable."

"I wouldn't dream of using one myself. The final

reworking is so important. Of course for some work it hardly matters."

His jaw muscle was hopping like a Mexican jumping bean; his voice was as thin and taut as a wire. "Shall we go back to the living room, or would you like to see the rest of the place?"

"I've seen enough, thanks. I can imagine the rest—mirrored ceiling in the master bedroom, fur coverlet, a billiards room tucked away somewhere." Stop it, Audrey! Stop now, before you go too far.

"I don't play billiards," he said in an arctic voice, as we went back to the living room. I got a glimpse of the dining room in passing. It had a large oval table surrounded by a dozen or so carved chairs. There was a baroque silver epergne on the table.

"Quite a collection," was my faint praise.

"I don't intend to apologize for what I've got. I earned it," he said simply.

"Then it's true you never go broke underestimating the taste of the public. Now, what are we going to do about Drew Taylor?" I asked, in a brisk businesslike manner.

"We came here to change. Let's do it, and discuss plans over dinner."

"It slipped my mind—your little French restaurant. You should have had it set up in your dining room, Brad. It'd save you even more time."

"Dining out is one of my simple pleasures," he said, still with an effort at civility. Then he added, "I'll show you to the guest room."

I followed him back down the hall to a room across from the library. It was done in Wedgwood blue, with white French furnishings. There was a bathroom en suite with a blue sunken tub and a chandelier.

"It came with the apartment," he said, when I slanted a look up at the chandelier.

"It saved you the bother of having it installed. I'll be ready in fifteen minutes. I can find my way back to the saloon. Hang a right at the end of the hall, I think?"

"That's one way. Or you can take the scenic route, hang a left just before you get to Zeus. It takes you through the conservatory," he retaliated, and walked out, his posture rigid.

If ever a visit was calculated to activate my feelings of inadequacy, this was it. Helen's condo was a slum compared to this. Even the showerhead got in on the act. It was brass-plated—or gold for all I knew—and had about a dozen choices of spray. My own had two, slow drizzle and off. I selected the massage button and stood under a swirling barrage of water needles, trying to relax as the water beat against my back and across my knotted shoulder blades.

I was tempted to climb back into my blue jeans for the trip to Le Pavillon d'Antibes. When you can't compete, the next best way is to mock the competitor's efforts. But my jeans were a mess from the trip. They looked as if I were still in them, every wrinkle and crease deeply set; so I wore the white suit again, with my hair hanging loose, falling straight as a ruler to my shoulders.

The face confronting me in the mirror looked rebellious. There were circles under my eyes from the trip, and my hair looked awful. Did He who made Brook Shields make me? I tried to twist my hair up, but didn't have enough pins to hold it. It only made me more annoyed.

"Now isn't that original, we're going as the Bobbsey twins!" I exclaimed, when I saw Brad had on a white suit too. Actually he looked fantastic. He had enough panache to wear the suit without looking ridiculous.

He refused to argue. "I can change if you like."

A momentary weakness assailed me; for about thirty seconds, I wanted to stop being such a bitch. "I was going to do my hair up, but I didn't have enough pins."

His stiff jaws relaxed into an incipient smile. "Don't change a hair for me."

"I'm a mess, Brad. You won't want to be seen in public with me."

"I can probably drum up a few pins if you want to . . ."

Another spurt of anger came upon me. Not because he failed to disagree about my being a mess, but because of the pins. What was he doing with hairpins if he didn't entertain women here—entertain them in a way that made them let their hair down? The unreasonableness of my anger only made me madder still.

"I won't bother." I flopped my hair back over my shoulder. "The place is probably dark anyway."

It was still daylight outside, however. "It's a bit early for dinner," he mentioned. "Too bad we got dressed. There's a pool on the roof."

I widened my eyes in mock amazement. "You mean there's none here, in your own apartment?"

If you've ever seen a woman defending her housekeeping to her mother-in-law, you know the expression on Brad's face. I watched as it hardened to rebellion. "Just the Jacuzzi. I usually spend my summers at Martha's Vineyard. My place there has a pool. I have a few calls to make. Do you think you could entertain yourself for half an hour?"

"Sure, just lead me to the games room."

"Your game is writing. I thought you'd like to browse in the library, or try out the computer. You'll be getting one yourself eventually, I imagine."

"I wouldn't dream of it, but I'll browse around the library."

Rifling through friends' bookshelves is one of my

favorite things to do. You discover such interesting keys to
a person's mind by the books he keeps. Brad's bookshelves
were so organized and so broad in scope that they told me
nothing, except that he was ashamed to have his Hume
Mason works on display. There wasn't a single copy in
evidence. *The Art of Eliot* was there, in all its Moroccan-
leather-and-gold-trim glory. There had to be one corner
where he kept the tattered old paperbacks and clothbound
ugly-but-wonderful books every writer I ever met keeps. In
my own case this shelf was the most crowded in my
apartment. *South Wind* was crammed in cheek by jowl with
a cherished copy of the *Sheik*. Still a great read after all
these years. There should be faded copies of old essays and
poetry anthologies, of joke books and books of little-known
facts.

A man who read as much as Brad O'Malley had to have
a collection like that. He just had them hidden away behind
a door, since they didn't match his decor. I opened a few
cabinet drawers and came across his cache. Tattered,
dog-eared books—a wonderful collection of miscellany.
The *DeQuincey Essays*, old English novels by women who
called themselves Mrs. Oliphant, or Mrs. McStead, instead
of using their own Christian names. More than one by "An
Englishwoman"—ladies who had traveled abroad to India
and the east with their menfolk. Emily Eden was there.
Rather a concentration of books by women actually.

I opened another cabinet door, and came across an even
more surprising batch of books. These were brand new, and
consisted of twenty or thirty thick paperback historical
romances with passionate covers and the title in writhing
gold letters—those sandwiches of sex and history that
invariably hurtle to the top of booklists. Rosalie Wildewood's *Love Last Longing* is a good example. In fact, there
were three of Rosalie's earlier books here. My lips thinned

in amusement to consider this ammunition. The intellectual lover of Popper and Eliot was a closet reader of women's historical romance.

Further rooting discovered nothing else of interest. I never did find his Hume Mason books. I just went to the sofa and looked idly around at the library, and through the open door into the office. It was unreasonable for me to be jealous of Brad's financial success. It never bothered me that other writers no more talented had achieved the rarified, seven-figure atmosphere. Brad had promised not to write his book on Rosalie, so why did it sting like a nettle that he had this fantastic apartment, his summer place at Martha's Vineyard, his artworks, everything?

Was it that his material things removed him to that charmed circle beyond the touch of mere mortals like Audrey Dane? The only intersection of our lives was Rosalie Hart. If I hadn't been doing a book on her, I'd never have met Brad O'Malley. His female friends would be models and actresses, successful designers and performers. Maybe a college professor or two, for variety.

The sun refused to set. It was still bright as afternoon, and it was nearly seven o'clock. Our appointment with Drew was for nine. How many phone calls was he making anyway? While I impatiently lit a cigarette, the phone in his office rang. I assumed it was an extension, and he'd answer it in another room. When it rang the third time, it occurred to me it might be a separate business phone, so I ran in and picked up the receiver. Brad must have lifted the extension at the same time. I heard him say "Brad O'Malley here." I lowered the receiver, but before it reached the cradle, a woman's purring voice stopped my hand.

"Darling, you're back. It took you long enough!" My conscience went slack. I should have hung up, but I put the receiver to my ear and eavesdropped. That voice sounded vaguely familiar.

"How'd the interview go, Rosalie?" Another Rosalie! That name—a fairly unusual name, too—kept cropping up with monotonous regularity. I felt my scalp prickle, as the identity of the caller dawned on me. It was Rosalie Wildewood! Brad actually knew her! That's why he had her books.

"You didn't see me?" It was all I could do to keep from blurting out that I'd seen her. She looked marvelous, and I loved *Love's Last Longing*.

"I had to go to L.A. How'd it go? Did you get a good plug in for the latest book?"

"I was fantastic. At least everyone tells me so. Will I be seeing you tonight, darling?"

"I'm tied up tonight, Rosalie."

"Did you have any success with Dane? Or need I ask?" she added, and laughed. "She *is* a woman, after all."

"I'll call you tomorrow," he said, very hurriedly.

"I'll be out all day. Autographing sessions at Dalton's and various shopping malls. Maybe we can get together for a drink after your dinner date tonight."

"We'll see. Bye."

I waited for the click of Brad's receiver. What I heard was his voice in my ear. "You can hang up now, Audrey."

I set the receiver on the cradle, wondering if he really knew I'd been listening, or was only guessing. I felt a perfect fool, but before I had much time to think about it, he was at the door, with the keys jangling in his fingers. He looked wary—it would be the matter of his "handling Dane" that accounted for it. As Dane had "handled" him, however, I didn't mean to rub his nose in it.

"It's early, but we'd better go if we want to be on time at Drew's place," he said.

"I thought your office phone was probably a separate listing. When you didn't answer, I just . . ."

"My life's an open book to you now. I guess you figured out that was Rosalie Wildewood on the phone?"

"Yes. Odd you didn't mention knowing her, when we talked about her earlier."

"I had the idea you thought I was always bragging, so I kept quiet. I met her at a booksellers' convention a few years ago. We see each other once in a while."

"What's she really like?" I asked, with all the enthusiasm of a groupie.

"She's a smart lady. Good-looking, too."

The car threaded slowly through the evening traffic to a side street on the Upper East Side. Le Pavillon wasn't a large restaurant, but the dimness of the lights and the quantity of jacketed flunkies alerted me that it wasn't cheap either. There was some obéissance to the French name in the fin-de-siècle elegance of chandeliers, red upholstery, and French paintings.

The maître d' made a fuss over Brad, and sent off a waiter to alert Chef Pierre *le patron* was here. I looked around the room while Brad and the sommelier discussed wines, and told him I'd have whatever he recommended. To betray the least interest in, or approval of, the place was unthinkable.

Dinner was good, but no better than we'd had at Brad's cottage, and certainly not as enjoyable. I kept harking back, in my mind, to the cottage, and to what Rosalie Wildewood had said. His "handling Dane" obviously meant getting at my research. "After all, she *is* a woman." That was why he'd courted me, then. Not that I didn't know it already, but to have others know was humiliating. I hardly even glanced at Brad. I felt the dark-eyed, handsome man sitting across from me was a stranger.

To break the silence, we reverted to the subject of Drew Taylor, and what we should do about getting back my painting.

"I hope she has the polka dot nude at her apartment," Brad said. "We need some hard evidence. We can verify it's the one that was stolen from your cottage."

"Then what—we call the police?"

"We take it to an expert and get his verification that it's not a genuine Pissarro, or whatever. That's what she'll try to pass it off as—probably a Pissarro. Then we call in the police to nab her books, and follow up on some of her other sales."

"If she makes a regular business of selling Rosalie's works for originals, the only one who can prove it is Lorraine Taylor, and they must be in on it together."

"Your nude ties the racket to Rosalie. Even if we can't prove where she got the other pictures, we can prove they're forgeries. The signed names will give it away."

This line of conversation got us through dinner. It wasn't a very enjoyable meal, but at least I wasn't bitchy. Brad invited me to the kitchen after dinner to congratulate Pierre, but I declined. I didn't want to know anything more about him and his interesting, full life. It would only be that much more to regret after the affair was over. And it was so close to being over!

CHAPTER 14

We got into the car for the short drive to Drew's apartment. At nine on the dot, the doorman announced us, and we were allowed to ascend to the penthouse, where a smiling Drew met us at the door. Her smile diminished when she saw I was along.

"Oh, Miss Andrews, you're here too," she exclaimed, letting her surprise show. She had a conscious air of doing it on purpose, to make me feel unwanted.

I knew Drew hadn't got herself rigged out in such an elaborate outfit just to show a client a picture. It was a sort of shift, slit from the guggle to the zatch. The material was a thick white crepe, edged in a gold key, Grecian ribbon. A heavy gold medallion, slightly smaller than a saucer, hung from a gold chain.

She led us into a large, square living room that was painted stark white, from ceiling to floor, where a white fur rug nuzzled our feet. The lamps were white; the sofas were white; any item such, as a table, that wasn't white was made of glass, to show white on all sides. I felt as if I'd fallen into a very large glass of milk. It was a dazzling setting for the paintings that bedizened the walls. Ruby reds, sapphire blues, emerald greens, and vibrant golds glowed above their individual lights, the thick blobs of impasto creating an interesting texture. There was a good representation of modern artists, some of the same ones already met on Brad's walls.

I recognized the style of Rouault, with thick leadlike lines of black. Drew's Rouault was a clown. Le´ger was represented in a machine man. The fake Matisse was lovely, the largest of the lot, of a woman sprawling on a sofa by a wicker table, with pots of flowers behind her. We hardly glanced at any of them. While Drew led us around from painting to painting, our eyes scoured the walls for the polka dot nude. It wasn't there. These other paintings were very likely the work of Rosalie, but the one we were after was not to be seen. While Brad chatted Drew up, I went close to the Rouault and examined the signature. If it had been altered, it had been so well done that the layman couldn't tell. While they admired the "Matisse," I began to figure how I could see the rest of the apartment. The bedroom, for instance, might have a few artworks.

"Ah, this one's a lovely painting, it is," Brad crooned in his best brogue. A fatuous smile dripped from his face.

"You have excellent taste, Timothy," Drew congratulated. "You've chosen the prize of my collection. I hadn't planned to sell it. It was the Modigliani I thought you might care for. Also a nude," she pointed out.

I expected that whatever painting he showed an interest in would be one she didn't want to sell, to raise the price.

Brad obligingly turned his eyes to the Modigliani, but was soon looking at the Matisse again. "That's a nude and no mistake. A wonderful light, playful touch he has, Matisse."

I jiggled Drew's elbow. "Excuse me, but could I use the bathroom?"

She didn't show alarm, or anything but slight annoyance. "Just down the hall," she said motioning. When I left, she was still extolling the virtues of Matisse. Brad angled himself so that she had to turn her back to the hall to talk to him.

Her bedroom was another marshmallow world, all white on white, but the three paintings there were smaller and less well executed than those in her living room. I took a quick peek under her bed and in her clothes closet, finding not a single speck of dust, and a fortune in designer labels, respectively, but no painting. The bathroom was tiled in dark burgundy tiles, and had more towels than the linen department of Bloomies, but it didn't have any paintings. Fresh flowers were the artwork in there.

When I returned, they had got down to haggling over the Matisse. "It's a fine painting, but I always had a weakness for softer, pastel shades," he said, hinting to hear whether she had a pastel polka dot nude without quite saying it.

"I don't have anything like that at the moment. Leave me your address in Ireland, Tim, and I'll let you know if I come across anything. Meanwhile, about the Matisse . . ." It seemed her reluctance to sell had been overcome.

I assumed Brad would now back out gracefully, but he said, "What are you asking for it?" His eyes caressed the nude's outlines, and Drew slanted a calculating glance at his profile.

"If I'd been able to get authentication papers with it, I could name my own price," she said ruefully. "Of course there's no doubt as to its authenticity," she added hastily. "It's signed—you can see for yourself. A man of your knowledge in these matters, Timothy, wouldn't have to look at the signature. The museums, however, like to have their paintings documented, so I could only sell it privately. That cuts down the price to a really ridiculous one, but you have to realize you'd have trouble if you planned to resell."

There was a longish silence. My shoulders tensed, but when Brad spoke, he said, "Oh, I'd never sell the likes of this lady," in his best Barry Fitzgerald brogue. I looked at Drew, and saw a small smile settle on her lips. She looked like a cat heading for the cream jar. "Where I'd put her is in my bedroom, alongside my Bonnard," Brad decided.

Drew looked indecisive. "I'm tempted to let it go. It's rare to find a true appreciator. You'd be surprised how many people only buy as an investment. Well, to name a figure—say, sixty-five thousand," she suggested, rather tentatively.

"It's the lack of documentation that bothers me a little," Brad said. "Who did you buy it from, if you don't mind my asking?"

"Unfortunately the previous owner is dead. I picked it up at an estate sale in Florida two years ago. The woman only had two decent paintings—the majority of the sale was jewelry, so that the art buyers weren't out en masse. I confess I only paid twenty-five thousand myself. It was Mrs. Julien Fairchild," she said, and looked closely at Brad.

"I'm not familiar with the name," he admitted. "I don't follow the American art dealings closely at all. I know what I like, as folks say, and that's good enough for me."

"This is a beautiful painting."

"No question of it, but the price . . . Say I give you fifty thousand cash on the nose for it. You've doubled your profit in two years."

"I'm sorry, Timothy. I turned down that price two months ago. I couldn't let it go for less than sixty thousand."

"Fifty-five," he countered.

After a very brief consideration, she said, "Agreed!" and

shook his hand. "It is lovely, isn't it?" She smiled fondly at
the painting as they went on talking for a few minutes.

"I'll make it easy for you," she said. "I'll wrap it up
myself and ship it to Ireland for you, no extra cost. We ship
many of our paintings abroad. The sheiks are snapping up
everything. We wrap them well in moisture-proof, damage-
proof containers. It'll save you carting it off to Kentucky.
I'll register and insure it, of course."

"I have a fancy to take to home with me to my hotel room
tonight," he said.

"There's the matter of payment . . ."

"You're right, of course. Why should you trust a
stranger? I'll have the certified check at your gallery in the
morning. Could you take the picture there, to save me
coming here for it? Say, ten in the morning."

"That will be no trouble at all. Now let's celebrate with
a drink!"

A bottle of champagne was already nestling in ice, with
two glasses on the table beside it. Delighted with her sale,
Drew had no aversion to producing another glass. I sat
silent as a jug while Drew and Brad carried on a bantering
flirtation. Before we left, he had a date to meet her for
dinner the next evening at Le Pavillon d'Antibes. I assumed
he had no intention of keeping this date, or he would have
chosen a place where he wasn't recognized at a glance as
Brad O'Malley.

As we went down the elevator I said, "Why on earth did
you buy that Matisse?"

"You didn't find the nude in her bedroom, did you?"

"Of course not, but her selling you a Matisse doesn't
prove she stole my nude."

"If the signature's been changed from Rosalie to Matisse,
it'll prove something."

"Yeah, it'll prove Barnum was right. I bet my nude's

down at her gallery, hidden in a back room somewhere. Fifty-five thousand dollars, Brad. Are you sure you'll be able to get it back? You can't stop payment on a certified check."

"She won't dare cash it when we're finished with her. She'll be happy to hand over your polka dot nude, just to keep us quiet. Want to go out and celebrate?"

"Celebrate what? So far we haven't done anything but waste fifty-five thousand dollars." This was intended as a comment only, not a refusal to go out, Brad decided to take offense. He was stiff and quiet for a while. When he drew near to Central Park West, I said, "I might as well go to my own apartment. Do you mind driving me across town?"

"I thought we'd go to my place first. You left your bag there," he reminded me, but in a careless way, not showing any disappointment. He was probably delighted he'd be getting home early enough to call Rosalie Wildewood.

"I can get it tomorrow. I have lots of clothes at home. Shall I meet you at the gallery at ten?"

"It'll save driving over to pick you up."

Brad offered not a word of discouragement to my plan. The car slid up in front of the dilapidated brownstone duplex. "I'll go in with you to make sure you haven't been taken over by squatters," he offered.

At my door, he waited just inside till I turned the lights on. "My God, you've been burgled here, too!" he exclaimed.

I looked calmly at the welter of confusion. "This is the way I left it. I packed in a bit of a hurry. I'll tidy it up now. Thanks for the lift. For everything, I mean."

"You're welcome." He stood with his arms folded on his chest, which gave him an air of permanence as though he meant to stay an hour or two. There was an angry question in his eyes, and a stubborn set to his chin.

"See you tomorrow," I said, edging him toward the door. "Goodnight." I softly closed the door. The Gucci loafer didn't slide in to hold it open. The Gucci loafer was probably on the gas pedal, rushing toward Rosalie Wildewood.

CHAPTER 15

I turned and looked at my apartment with the eye of a disinterested observer. You could tell to look at it the person who lived here had an ego the size of pea, and the domestic instincts of a hobo. There was no reason it had to look like a garage sale, just because the carpet was nylon, instead of one hundred percent wool, hand knotted in the Orient. I should have gotten busy and cleaned it up, but first I wanted to do some thinking. I personally can't think when I'm dressed up in a white suit that wrinkles if you look at it. I got into my thinking clothes, jeans and a jersey, sat on the sofa with my knees pulled under me, and thought about the situation.

My typewriter ribbon suggested the polka dot nude had been shipped to Drew Taylor at her apartment. It wasn't at her apartment, and I didn't think she'd had time to sell it. It had to be at her shop. All I had to do to get it back was to get into her shop—tonight—and retrieve it, and I'd save Brad fifty-five thousand dollars. Better yet, I'd show him that while he was an ineffectual dilettante, I was an achiever. I might live in a pigsty; I might not get six-figure advances for my books, but I was more of a man than he was. My shriveled ego demanded some satisfaction, and the author of two preteen mysteries knew what was required of her heroine. I was scared stiff, but my conscience was already dulled from my former breaking and entering of Brad's cottage.

The trouble with breaking into her gallery was that I couldn't do it from the front, where I'd be seen, and I was scared out of my gourd to go into some back alley alone at night. I didn't own a gun, or even a can of Mace. The preferred accomplice for the job was a strong man, but Garth was in Greece—though he might possibly be back by now. He knew clever lawyers, which would come in handy if we were caught. And he wasn't a chicken by any means. Helen would never marry a chicken. But Garth would be all for handing the affair over to the authorities; he'd want me to get a search warrant and sensible things like that. Upon further reflection, I was coming to convince myself Garth wasn't so great after all. He didn't own a restaurant, Rosalie Wildewood didn't call him "Darling," and he didn't have much of a sense of humor either. What I needed was a very brave fool. What I needed was . . . Jerome Hespeler.

Jerome and I had gone to high school and college together. We two introverted misfits were good, old friends. Jerome ran a children's bookstore that stocked my preteen mysteries. Compared to him, I was a roaring success. He admired me, and would give his bifocals for a chance to break and enter with me. He was about the only man I could phone after ten o'clock at night, too. I called. Jerome was at home, and yelped delightedly that he'd be right over.

I did a quick cleanup of the pigsty, and met Jerome at the door within half an hour. Jerome wears the aforementioned bifocals and is only an inch taller than I am, but his arms are strong enough, and he's really quite ingenious. I outlined my problem to him, with many interruptions.

"You really met Rosalie Hart. Wow, what an experience, Aud."

"It's her daughter's gallery I want to break into."

"Breaking and entering—just like TV."

"Except if we get caught, we go to a real jail."

"We might be on TV." He beamed foolishly. "Your publishers would get us out of jail—wouldn't they?"

"They'd probably love the publicity. And I'm not the real thief."

Once he was convinced I was a victim, we discussed ways and means of getting into the gallery. Jerome used to drive a taxi before he got to be manager of the bookstore, and knows every street and alley in New York. What we decided to do was drive past the gallery, looking for the closest alley. He'd park his Volkswagon Beetle in the alley, and we'd go scouting from there.

He had the foresight to bring a toolkit containing things like hammers, screwdrivers, wrenches, and two flashlights. The closest alley to Drew's gallery wasn't even on the same street, but around a corner. He drove down to the end of the alley, turned off the lights, and parked. We slipped out and went hand in hand along a narrower passage till we came to a strip of land about four yards wide, with a fence at the side.

"The gallery is the third shop from the corner. We'll have to hop that fence, and maybe another," Jerome whispered. "There might be dogs," he added, with a certain relish. If a Doberman pinscher came baring his teeth at me, I meant to retire at top speed; but till I saw whether or not we had dogs to contend with, I didn't confess it. We clambered over the fence. From there, it was surprisingly easy. There was no other fence. There were two doors. The last, according to Jerome, was Drew's. It was locked by an old-fashioned padlock. I held the flashlight while Jerome unscrewed the whole mechanism from the door. After that, there was nothing to do but walk in. Our flashlights showed us a narrow passage into a storage room.

"There might be an alarm system," was Jerome's next effort to give me a heart attack.

"I doubt it. Her stuff is hardly worth stealing. Wouldn't we have heard it anyway?"

"It wouldn't ring here—it'd ring at the police station. Let's see, the closest station is five blocks away. We have less than ten minutes, Audrey," he said calmly.

"You take a look in the next room. I'll look here."

He already knew what we were looking for. I went with him, to make sure the area he was searching was the same room Brad and I had seen that afternoon. It was Drew's office, and large enough that the painting could be concealed somewhere. While he looked there, I went back to the store room.

It was littered with old wooden frames, some of them heavily carved. There was a table holding cans of gold spray paint and other, nonaerosol cans, along with brushes, old rags, hanging wire, and a few tools. This was where Drew mounted the canvases onto frames for display.

Against one wall stood some garish abstract expressionist paintings like the ones in the front gallery. I began lifting them aside, one by one, with a definite feeling of repetition. One explosion of lines after another. My ears were perked for the keening of a police siren. That's what I was listening for—a loud noise from the distance. I hardly paid any attention to closer, smaller sounds. At least that's my excuse. When the man came silently up to the back door, I didn't hear a thing, not so much as the padding of a foot. The first intimation that we had company was the turning of the doorknob. My heart jumped into my throat. I turned off

my flashlight and stood shaking in my Adidas. Jerome! Had
he heard the knob turn?

It was dark in the room, *really* dark, no moonlight or
anything. I couldn't see who had come in, but I knew from
the way the floor moved that it was a fairly big man. A
policeman? A henchman of Drew's? Some other quite
disinterested criminal, like a murderer or rapist, maybe? I
didn't move a muscle—I didn't swallow, I don't think I
breathed—while the man tiptoed past me, into Drew's
office. He knew we were here— he'd have seen that the
lock was taken off the back door. Since he knew we were
here, and wasn't afraid, he obviously had a gun. And unless
TV lied, police didn't enter the scene of a crime in this
surreptitious manner. They kicked in doors and yelled,
"Freeze!" The man was not a cop, so by induction he was
a robber. Great—Jerome was going to end up with a bullet
in his chest because I wanted to impress Brad O'Malley.

I didn't want to turn on my flashlight, but I had to find a
weapon, something to hit the intruder over the head with,
when I crawled up behind him. At least he was alone; it was
two against one. I edged to the work table and felt around
in the dark till my fingers closed over cold metal. A
hammer—good enough. I'd have to tap gently or I'd kill
him. All was silent in the next room. Jerome must have
heard the man and turned off his flashlight. With luck, the
man might pass straight through to the front gallery.

I crept quietly to the door and listened. Not a sound.
You'd have sworn the room was unoccupied, till the
intruder turned on a flashlight. I knew it was the intruder
and not Jerome, because he was only two feet inside the
door. In the light's beam, I saw Jerome's bifocals twinkle.
I expect I imagined the look of terror in the eyes behind the
glasses, but it would have been there all the same. I raised
the hammer and struck, firmly but not fatally hard, at where

the intruder's head should have been. He was taller than I thought. I just grazed his ear and the side of his head. It should have been enough to knock him out, but certainly not kill him. I was glad, as long as he was knocked out.

"Come on," I called to Jerome.

"What about him?" Jerome asked.

"Never mind him. I didn't kill him."

"I wonder who he is," Jerome said, and played his light on the fallen hulk.

For an instant, I had the strange impression the man had disappeared. There didn't seem to be anything on the floor where he had fallen. I turned my light to him, too, and discovered a black lump, totally, absolutely jet black from head to toe. He wore a black ski mask, a long-sleeved black jersey, black gloves, black trousers, and black sneakers. A special color-coordinated outfit for breaking and entering. My curiosity was piqued, and when Jerome leaned over to lift the mask, I didn't stop him, which proved to be a mistake.

The black lump came to life. Jerome was suddenly pulled to the floor and flung aside. The lump leapt out and pounced on me. Being only human, I opened my mouth and howled in mortal terror. A black leather glove clamped over my mouth, and I was restrained against a concrete chest. I hoped Drew had an alarm, and that police cars would soon arrive, sirens wailing.

The lump swore off a string of curses, ending in the word "Audrey?" in a questioning tone.

I might have known who would get himself rigged out in a matching outfit to go breaking and entering. "Brad, is that you?"

He let go. "What are you doing here?"

"What do you think? Jerome, are you all right?" I turned my light on him.

Jerome picked himself up from the floor, adjusting his glasses and rubbing his left arm. "I think so. And Audrey, we really should be getting out of here. The police might come any minute."

"Jerome thinks there might be an alarm," I explained.

"Did you find it?" Brad asked.

I knew he meant the picture, not the alarm. "No."

"Is this it?" Jerome inquired politely, and went to a corner to hold up my polka dot nude, still in her gilt frame, and still as lovely as ever.

"You found it!" I squealed, and ran to make sure it was my picture. The only difference was that the name *Rosalie* had been changed to *Pissarro*.

"Good, let's blow," Brad suggested, and we left.

"What about the lock?" Jerome asked.

"Drew's going to know she'd had company when this is gone. There's no point trying to hide we were here," I pointed out. As about nine and a half minutes had elapsed since we went in, Jerome didn't argue.

"Did you drive here?" Jerome asked Brad.

"No, I took a cab, and stopped a block away."

"Can I give you a lift?"

"I'd appreciate it."

Brad squeezed himself into the backseat of the Volkswagon Beetle and we left. There was no sign of police cruisers, no sound of sirens. I don't think Drew had any alarm at all, but we didn't stay around to find out if the police came later.

"Where to?" Jerome asked.

"My place is the closest," I said. "How's your head, Brad?"

"Speak up. I can't hear you very well. My left ear's bleeding."

We all went to my apartment. Jerome made coffee while

I bandaged Brad's ear. It wasn't really his ear that was bleeding. The skin was gouged above the ear, and a little trickle of blood oozed down—nothing desperate, though he tried to make me feel guilty.

"I can't put a Band-Aid on this unless you let me shave a bit of your hair off," I explained.

"Shave my hair? You're crazy! Elaine would have a fit."

"A lady friend?"

"My hairdresser. No Band-Aid. Use a bandage."

"You just want to look like van Gogh. I'll put some antiseptic on it."

I got the peroxide bottle and daubed some on with a cotton swab. A patch of white foam bubbled up above his ear, while howls of painful protest bellowed from his mouth.

"You're torturing me to death!"

"It's only peroxide."

"Peroxide? Oh my God, I'll have blond streaks in my hair."

"A fate worse than poverty. Elaine can touch it up for you. Here, wipe off that foam. You look like a mad dog." It had slid down and was gathering on his chin.

"You're a cruel woman, Audrey. No feminine compassion. You haven't even said you're sorry for hitting me with a hammer."

"I'm sorry. And you haven't told me why you were there."

"We were both there for the same reason."

"You didn't say you were going."

"Neither did you."

"I was trying to save you fifty-five thousand bucks."

"All we've done is tip her off," he lamented. "Not that she can do much about it, except report the picture as stolen."

"Which she won't, since she stole it from me in the first place. What do you think we should do now? I mean are you still going to her gallery tomorrow morning?"

"Oh yes, I'm still going . to buy the Matisse. The difference is, I won't have to pay for it."

"Coffee's ready," Jerome called, and brought the pot into the living room. "Well, this was quite a night." He smiled happily. "We haven't done anything like this for a long time, Aud."

Brad cast a curious look from Jerome to me. One could wish Jerome had been six inches taller, and a little less emaciated, since the look suggested Brad took him for a boyfriend. A T-shirt that didn't have Kermit the Frog's picture on it would have helped, too. Actually the only other criminal activity Jerome and I ever undertook together was painting the math teacher's windows one Halloween.

"Remember the night we painted old Johnson's windows?" Jerome smiled.

Jerome did a lot of smiling the next half hour, as he regaled Brad with long and boring stories of our youthful exploits in drama clubs and minor student revolts. It brought home graphically how extremely tedious my life had been. By eleven-thirty neither of them gave any indication they had a home to go to.

"Well, it's getting late," I said, and stretched my arms sleepily.

"Yeah; hey, did Aud ever tell you about the time we fell out of the canoe?" Jerome asked Brad.

"Yeah, she told me that one," Brad lied, and laughed in spurious memory. "Right in the water."

"With all her clothes on," Jerome added.

I yawned ostentatiously. "I don't know about you guys, but I have to get up early in the morning."

"You can get up whenever you want to. You writers—

boy, you really have it made," Jerome said, and reached for the coffeepot. Fortunately, it was empty.

"You still have to be in the store at nine, Jerome," I reminded him. "I don't want to keep you too late. Thanks a lot for helping me."

"Anytime. Can I give you a lift, Brad?"

Brad looked a question at me. "It'll save calling a cab," I told him. His black eyes skewered me.

They finally left. I bolted the door and sat smiling at my painting. I'd gotten it back, which was my major concern, but I knew Brad planned to go on and solve the whole mystery. Since it involved Rosalie and my book, it concerned me too—actually more so than Brad. I began to wonder why he was still following it up at all. We'd only come here to recover my painting, and we'd done that, but the predatory gleam in his eye told me he had no notion of letting up.

CHAPTER 16

How we were going to proceed in the morning was unclear, now that I had my polka dot nude. Why, for instance, had Brad said he was still going to buy the Matisse? Did he expect me to meet him at the gallery, polka dot nude in hand, or were we to hide from Drew that I had it? When I figured Brad had had time to get home, I called him. There was no answer. That was at midnight. He still wasn't home at twelve-thirty, or at one. By one-thirty, I wouldn't have spoken to him if he came dashing up to my door on a white charger.

I spent the wakeful hours between one and three A.M. deciding how I could remove from my life this toothache named Brad O'Malley, who was certainly out with Rosalie Wildewood, giving her new ideas for her famous love scenes. Having come to New York in his car, I would either have to bus it back to the cottage, or hire a car and drive myself. That would be the first little hint that I didn't care for his company. I doubted that he planned to remain on at Simcoe's cottage now that he wasn't writing his Rosalie book, but if it transpired that he planned to remain, I would leave. I would not go on having my life turned upside down by him. Meanwhile, in the morning I would dress and behave like a civilized human being. I would be witty and charming, yet devastatingly disinterested. I would smile, I would say "I hope you slept well," with no emphasis whatsoever on the word "slept."

My apartment was a humid ninety degrees when I woke up. My blue tailored dress with crisp white trim had lost its crispness. My hair had lost everything except its straightness. But I refused to be depressed. I did my best with the hair, put on the dress, and added ivory jewelry in recognition that it was summer in the city.

By nine I was ready—a mere hour too early. That happens when you get out of bed at seven. I called Brad again, expecting either no answer, or a woman's voice. "Brad, it's me," I announced brightly. "I hope I didn't get you out of bed."

He sounded heavy with sleep. "No," he said. "I meant to call you."

"I was just wondering if you want me to bring along my painting this morning."

"No! Don't tip her off. We'll leave it in the car."

"But I'm taking a taxi."

"I'll pick you up."

My dress became a little crisper at this news. "All right. Did you get the certified check?"

"I'm picking it up on the way to your place."

"Why are you doing this, Brad?"

"To lull Drew's suspicions. I don't want her to do anything rash before we get your picture to an expert. Let's get there a little early, before she has time to discover her back door's open."

When Brad called for me, he wore dark glasses. "The top o' the morning to you, Mr. O'Casey." I smiled. "I bet they don't wear sunglasses in Ireland, Timothy me lad. You'll be giving yourself away."

"You're bright-eyed and bushy-tailed this morning," he said.

"I'm a terrible traveler. Being cooped up in a car all day made me surly yesterday. Sorry I inflicted it on you."

"I'm used to the rough side of your tongue by now," he said, and pulled off the sunglasses. His eyes were noticeably bloodshot.

"Better put them back on," I suggested. To my credit, I made none of the obvious suggestions as to how he'd acquired those inflamed eyes.

"Let's go. I'd like to catch Drew on her way into the gallery."

My painting was wrapped in a plastic garbage bag. We put it on the backseat and were waiting at Drew's door when she got there. She had the Matisse with her, already wrapped for its transoceanic voyage. Brad held it while she unlocked the door. "I can ship this to you in Ireland, and save your carrying it," she suggested once more.

"I'll take it along with me, but it was grand of you to wrap it up so well," he said.

"I wouldn't undo it till I got it home, if I were you. Just for safekeeping," she advised.

We went in and Brad drew the certified check out of his wallet. I peered at it over Drew's shoulder, smiling at the *Timothy O'Casey* written in Brad's big scrawl, all perforated and stamped and certified, and looking as official as a passport. Amazing what money could do.

There was an exchange of congratulations and thanks, a reminder of dinner that evening, and we were off, Brad carrying the wrapped painting.

"The first thing we have to do is unwrap it and make sure

she hasn't pulled a switch," I said urgently. "She was very insistent that you not unwrap it."

"That's not what she's up to. She just doesn't want anybody who might know something about art getting too close a look at it. We'll soon know. I've arranged for Art Whitdale at the Met to examine it."

We drove to Fifth Avenue, where Mr. Whitdale was waiting in his office. He was a tall, thin, elegant man with sandy hair and tinted glasses. When the Matisse was unwrapped, it was indeed the one that had hung in Drew's apartment the night before. We placed it beside my polka dot nude and Whitdale examined them both.

"Nice job. The colors are good," he said, nodding and removing his glasses to clarify the colors. He turned his attention to my nude. "The pointillism isn't as meticulous as Pissarro's would be. Still, it's a good forgery. Who did it?" He suggested a few names, none of them familiar to me.

"Rosalie Hart," Brad said.

Whitdale laughed. "No, seriously, where did you find these paintings?"

"At the Drew Taylor gallery."

"Did she have forged papers to go with them?" Whitdale asked. His nose was wiggling at the scent of a good scandal.

"No, she sold them 'as is.' "

"Really Brad, I thought you knew better!" Whitdale howled. "You'll have trouble nailing her down, if she didn't guarantee them for originals. She only has to say she mistook them for originals, and you don't have a leg to stand on. *Caveat emptor* and all that. What did you pay?"

"The Matisse was fifty-five thousand. What kind of a reputation does the gallery have in art circles?" Brad asked.

"She handles mostly young, upcoming artists. A few of them are good—well, promising at least. Quite frankly, I don't know how she pays the rent. I believe she's a rich lady amusing herself with a genteel hobby. You hear rumor occasionally of some older items she picks up at private sales, but none of the important collectors have bought from her, as far as I know. She doesn't even approach them. Are all of her items of this kind, I wonder?" Whitdale cocked a mobile brow at us.

"I imagine so, which accounts for her not peddling them to people who know something about art," Brad said.

"But you do. How were you taken in?" Whitdale asked. "You could have had a good copy painted for a tenth of that price, if all you wanted was a copy."

"It's not the forgery I'm interested in," Brad said. "The nude woman was stolen from Miss Dane."

"Ah, this is your writer friend you mentioned on the phone yesterday." Whitdale turned to me with sharper interest. "Charmed to meet you, Miss Dane."

After a little personal conversation, he reverted to business. "What is it you want of me, Brad?" he asked.

"I'd like you to have a go at the signatures and clean them off for us, with turpentine or whatever you use."

I felt a spasm of alarm. "Shouldn't we get a few witnesses first?"

That, for some reason, sent Brad into shock. "We want to keep this quiet. It might be a good idea to get a photograph though, Art. Do you have a camera?"

"We have a room set up for the purpose, with proper lighting and excellent cameras. I'll arrange it."

It was arranged and executed with all due pomp and ceremony. Mr. Whitdale took about a dozen pictures of both the "Matisse" and the nude; then we returned to his office to work on the signature.

"Shouldn't be too difficult. This one looks fairly fresh,"

Whitdale said, glancing at my nude. "I wonder what she used to age it. A pretty good match with the old pigments."

From a cupboard on the wall behind him, he got a bottle of colorless liquid, a stick with cotton swabs on the ends, and began carefully daubing at the black signature. It came away quite easily, while the paints hardened over the years stayed intact. In approximately five minutes, the word Rosalie was there, for all to see. The Matisse was next, with the same results.

"There you are," Art said. "Not a question about it. Do you want me to go to the gallery with you, Brad?"

"No, thanks, but I'd like to use your name to intimidate her."

"Feel free. I'd be happy to appear in court, if necessary. This is the kind of chicanery that gives art dealers a bad name. It makes people afraid to invest."

We exchange good-byes and assurances of meeting again, and took the paintings to the car.

"Drew's going to be surprised to see us land back in on her so soon," I mentioned. "Don't you think we should take a policeman along?"

"Let's hear what she has to say first. People have a way of clamming up with the formality of reading them their rights and the stern eye of the law on them."

"Whatever you say, but if she pulls a gun out of her desk, don't expect any heroics from me. I'm not that crazy about my picture."

"You were crazy enough about it last night to break into her shop. Why didn't you invite me along?"

"I'd imposed enough on your good nature. Make that so-so nature. Why didn't *you* invite *me*?"

He gave me a laughing look. "I wanted to outdo you, too. You never mentioned Jerome before."

"Jerome and I go way back—he's a good friend."

"Oh, the apples you've stolen together! The school play where he was Saint Joseph and you the Virgin Mary, dropping the baby doll back in kindergarten. It's unhealthy, living in the past, Audrey."

Not knowing what other items Jerome might have blabbed about in the car, I cut this line short. "What did you think when you saw the lock had been taken off Drew's door last night? Weren't you afraid to go in?"

"I had a strong feeling it would be you. Who else would be interested in that particular place, at that particular time? The beat-up Volkswagon convinced me. Only you would go breaking and entering, planning your getaway in a tin can thirty years old."

"At least we had wheels. It's better than relying on a taxi."

Drew was with another customer when we entered. She had her purse in her hand, and was leading him to the door, obviously preparing to run herself. She didn't look frightened; more angry, or frustrated. So she'd discovered the break-in then, and that the painting was gone then.

"Mr. O'Casey, have you decided to buy another of my paintings while you're passing through New York?" she asked ironically. Her topaz eyes had already taken note of the two paintings Brad carried, and the loose condition of their wrappings.

He waited till the other man left before he spoke, dropping the brogue now. "No, I'm dissatisfied with the one I bought this morning."

"Really! What seems to be the trouble?" Odd as it was, she seemed only curious, not afraid.

Brad put the Matisse on the counter and unfolded the paper. "It's this signature that bothers me," he said, and pointed to the word *Rosalie*. "And of course the fact that it's not a genuine Matisse."

Drew glanced at it, but her eyes soon strayed to the other painting, still in its cover. "I don't understand. How did this happen?" she asked.

"My friend—you must know Art Whitdale at the Met— discovered Rosalie Hart's signature lurking here under the other name. He feels that Matisse was added very recently—something about the state of pigment. He's ready to say so in court. You've had the thing two years, I think you said? Isn't that right, Miss Andrews? You can verify that claim?" I nodded.

Drew looked coolly from Brad to me. "What makes you think it's Rosalie Hart's signature? It only says Rosalie. It could be anyone."

"It's Rosalie Hart's. My friend here—actually her name is Miss Dane—was a friend of Rosalie's."

"Audrey Dane!" Drew exclaimed, and looked at me, finally taking more than a glance. "So that's who you are! I don't have to ask what's in the other parcel, do I? It's the nude she gave you."

"That's right, the one you had stolen from my cottage," I told her.

Her bold topaz eyes stared into mine, with a look as enigmatic as the Mona Lisa's. She wasn't quite smiling, but fear made up no part of her expression. "All right, let's talk. We'll be more comfortable in my office," she said, and led us to it. Brad picked up the paintings and brought them along.

"I noticed you've lost your accent, Mr. O'Casey," Drew mentioned. "Just where do you fit into the picture? As if I didn't know."

"You can consider me an interested party. Mostly I'm interested to know why you had the nude stolen."

"Stolen?" she asked, and laughed lightly. "Prove it. I bought it from a man who came in off the street a few days ago. If it's a forgery, I don't want it. You can keep it, Miss Dane. I'll give you back your check for the Matisse, Mr. O'Casey; you give me the painting, and we're square." She took the check from her purse and handed it to him.

"That'll do for starters," he said, and pocketed it. For a nervous minute, we all three looked uncertainly at each other. It was Brad who broke the silence. "The polka dot nude will make a great cover for your biography, Audrey. Not many people know what a great artist Rosalie was. How she worked with Braque, Rouault, and Picasso—all those artists in France. I wonder what happened to all her pictures. You wouldn't have any idea, Miss Taylor?"

"None," she said airily. "I hadn't heard Rosalie Hart was an artist. You interviewed her, Miss Dane. Did she say anything about her paintings?"

"Oh yes," I answered mysteriously.

"We took the idea some smart businesswoman got hold of them and sold them as originals," Brad said. "Fixed up the signature, shuffled them out of the country to some little-traveled corner of the world—like Ireland."

Drew's smile stretched wider. "Is that what you thought? I wish you luck in proving it, Mr. O'Casey."

"It shouldn't be too hard. The suspect's books can be seized and examined, some of the purchasers contacted. A search warrant to take the paintings that presently decorate her own apartment . . ."

"It's not against the law to hang anything I want on my own walls. I could hang a copy of *The Last Supper* and sign it 'da Vinci' without being arrested. And do you really suppose the seller was fool enough to keep records? I think it more likely she—or he—did it all under the table," Drew said. "No one got hurt in the transaction. The buyers got a beautiful, valuable work of art, at a bargain price. Unauthenticated, of course, which limits their trying to sell it.

They bought for their own enjoyment, and could afford it. And if you think they'll help you prove their bargain is a forgery, think again. No widows or orphans were fleeced in the process—so what's your problem?"

"One widow was robbed—Rosalie Hart."

Drew's face twisted into a bitter parody of a smile. "She was loaded. My mother was a slave to her for years, putting up with treatment no one else would take in these days."

"My mother"—Drew was saying Lorraine was her mother. Had Rosalie never told her the truth then, or was she trying to con us?

"She wasn't indentured," Brad pointed out. "She was free to go."

"Go where? Rosalie was her life."

"She could have come to you," Brad said. "Or did your mother have to stay with Rosalie to get the paintings from her? You've been defrauding Rosalie's estate for three years."

"Rosalie's estate was left to my mother, who is getting her fair share from the pictures. Don't be too sure Rosalie didn't have a hand in it too. At least I'll say so, if anyone is foolish enough to take it to court. Who can argue with a corpse?" she asked blandly. This struck me as a callous way to talk about her own mother.

"She never received a cent from your gallery!" Brad accused.

"How do you know, Mr. O'Casey?" Drew asked.

Brad blushed; Drew frowned, and I said, "What's going on here? I know perfectly well you're Rosalie's daughter, and I think it's disgusting . . ."

Drew threw her head back and laughed, a real, genuine belly laugh. "This is rich!" she said. "You're writing Rosalie's biography, and you don't know a damned thing about her. You be sure to print that I'm Rosalie's daughter,

Miss Dane. I'd love to sue your publisher for a couple of million."

"Brad, what's—" I stopped, hardly knowing what question to ask from the many that assailed me.

Brad and Drew were locked in a battle of eyes, staring at each other with curious determination. Again it was Brad who spoke. "Whatever the setup was, it's over. No more selling Rosalie's works as forged masterpieces."

"I never sold a thing as an authenticated original. Anyway, they're gone. What's left are the few you saw in my apartment."

"Fine, we'll take them, and call it settled," Brad said. "The word is out in the artistic community what kind of an operation you're running. You close shop, and that'll be the end of it."

"Very well, Mr. O'Malley."

"The name's O'Casey," Brad smiled.

"Sure, and mine's Shirley Temple. I'll send the paintings to Central Park West, but you don't broadcast what went on here, and that includes what you write in the book, Miss Dane."

Mysteries collided with enigmas in my mind. How did Drew know Brad's name, and his address? Why did she act as though she were bargaining from strength, when she didn't have a leg to stand on? Why wasn't she afraid of us, and why wasn't Brad going after her harder?

"The book's about Rosalie, not a painting fraud," Brad said. "Come on, Audrey, let's get out of here. I don't like the atmosphere."

"It was fine before you came in, Mr. O'Malley," Drew said. She lifted a pack of cigarettes and slowly lit one, with an insolent stare as we gathered up our paintings to leave.

CHAPTER 17

"How did she know who you are, and where you live?" I demanded, as we hurried to the parking lot.

"She's part witch."

"She must have heard Hume Mason was doing a book too," I reasoned. "How many people know Mason's real name anyway?"

With his eyes firmly riveted on the car, he replied, "Not many, and if Drew Taylor thinks *I'm* Mason, she isn't one of the select circle who knows."

"What do you mean, if she *thinks* you're Mason. You *are* Mason!"

"We'll do IDs later, okay?" he said brusquely, while he strode on his long legs to the car. "Did we let her off too easily?"

"*Now*, Brad. We'll do IDs now."

"That's a sit-down-and-have-a-drink story, Audrey. Trust me."

A busy parking lot seemed a poor spot to sit down and have a drink. "Okay, but you're not going to wiggle out of it this time."

"So, did we let her off too easily?" he repeated.

I allowed myself to be temporarily detoured to this topic. "We couldn't prove anything. Between her not keeping records and not authenticating the paintings, it'd be impossible to prove fraud. And as she said, her victims would be the last ones to help—they want to believe they have genuine masterpieces."

"I don't feel too sorry for them. They got what they paid for—famous names to hang on the wall and impress their friends."

"Some people are so interested in appearances," I agreed, slyly innocent, as we climbed into the Benz.

"Don't start on me, Audrey. It was her giving Rosalie a black eye that bothered me most. There'd be no way to prove Rosalie wasn't a part of the scheme."

"Maybe she was."

"No, she wasn't." A muscle at the side of his jaw quivered. Something was upsetting him, either the conversation, or the terrible job he was doing of getting the car into gear.

"How would *you* know? I didn't think she had a clue myself. She was growing senile. All she remembered was the movies, and the men, and the wild affairs. She just had that one painting of her own, in her bedroom. I wonder why she wanted me to have it."

"Didn't she say?"

"Well, she'd already told me about her painting, and that she was pretty good. I guess I didn't look convinced, so she showed it to me. I oohed and ahed, and she handed it over. Generous. She must have known she didn't have long to live. Maybe she wanted me to write nice things about her art, and considered the painting a bribe. I'm just conjecturing."

"Did Lorraine Taylor object?"

"She didn't know. She was upstairs that day, having a

rest. She might have objected after I left, but I wasn't aware of it. Maybe I *will* use the polka dot nude for a cover. I didn't agree not to—I just didn't disagree when Drew laid down the law. What do you think, Brad?"

"The dead deserve some privacy, and if this story gets out, Rosalie will be smeared with it. It's not much of a part of her life."

"It does detract from her real accomplishments—her movies."

"We have some unfinished business to discuss. I'm driving us back to my place, okay?" Brad said. I took it for a rhetorical question, as we were already headed in that direction.

"Mason's alter ego, you mean? Or should I say O'Malley's alter ego?"

"Since you're in a better mood today, I hoped we might make up for lost time last night. Jerome got in the way."

"Your bleeding eyes look as if you didn't waste much time last night. Didn't you call Rosalie Wildewood after all?"

"Jerome fed me a bottle of homemade wine. We talked till three or four. I know all your secrets now, Aud."

This came as a hard blow. Jerome knows me better than is comfortable. Many an afternoon he psychoanalyzed me in the college coffee shop, explaining why I shouldn't be jealous of Helen. When Helen got engaged to Garth, he was the one who dragged out all the old cliché's about plenty of fish in the sea.

"That nut? He doesn't know a neurosis from a neutron."

"He knows a lot about kid sisters, and inferiority complexes."

I bet he didn't know how I felt right now, as though my skin had been stripped off, and I stood with my raw nerve endings exposed. My old misgivings stormed over me when we entered the marble hallways, with Zeus towering at the end of it. I sat on the edge of the suede sofa, while Brad disposed of the paintings, before he joined me.

"I can see you're not exactly crazy about my place. What is it that turns you off?" he asked frankly.

"It's lovely. I don't know what you're talking about."

"It's as nice as I can make it. To tell the truth, I was hoping to bowl you over with it, but you grew a two-inch shell the minute you set foot in the door yesterday. And it's happening again." He stared hard, trying to read the answer on my stiffening face.

"I just hadn't pictured you living in a place like this." I glanced at the art-strewn walls. "You're not—I don't know. You're just not what I thought you were. You seem like a stranger here." I was dissatisfied with this trite speech, and so was Brad.

"It took me a while to get used to having money," he admitted, as his eyes followed mine around the room. "I didn't always live like this, but I always wanted to. I still do—my visit chez Simcoe convinced me of it. I used to live in a place like that when I was a professor. When my books started to earn a lot of money, I decided to spend it. Why not? I didn't have anyone to leave it to. I guess you knew my wife and son were fabrications, to give me an excuse to go to Rosalie's funeral." My shell began to soften. "Surely I don't have to apologize for making a success of my career, and enjoying the rewards? Won't you move up, when you make it?"

"I'll never make it this big. It's only trash that sells so well. Trash and sex. I can't understand how a professor of literature could lower himself," I challenged. As he defended himself against this charge, I began to doubt his disavowal regarding Mason.

He waved a dismissing hand. "Professors of literature

have to eat, too. I happen to like steak and wine. I prefer
Central Park West to a walk-up in some dark alley. I also
like having my audience numbered in millions, instead of
hundreds. *The Art of Eliot* sold nine hundred and seven
copies, six hundred in the college where it was put on the
curriculum for two years. When I left, the next professor
put his book on the syllabus. In my opinion, forcing kids to
buy your book is worse cheating than doing an honest
journeyman's job of work and letting the customer make his
own free choice. I am what I am, and I like doing what I do.
If you can't accept that . . ." He hunched his shoulders
indifferently, but his eyes still looked concerned. The crease
between his brows deepened, giving him an angry air.

"It's your business if you want a career of literary
prostitution," I said magnanimously.

"As opposed to the sort of literary worship you carry on!
Rummaging around in other people's lives, ferreting out
their secrets, making a pre´cis of their diaries and letters."

"Look who's talking!" I objected, voice rising several
decibels. "At least I have their permission, and I don't
pretend I was there in the room when Rosalie seduced her
lovers, panting right along, with the heaving bosoms and
shuddering loins. God, what rubbish! You should be
ashamed of yourself."

"I haven't been hauled into court for obscenity yet.
Bosoms *do* heave, Audrey; loins shudder, like it or not. The
days of trembling virgins are behind us. If you realized it
you might make a decent living yourself, instead of being
jealous and spiteful because I have." Brad's voice rose
above mine in volume.

"I'm not jealous of this furniture-store window. If you're
so insecure you have to bolster your ego with foreign cars
and a fancy address, that's your problem."

"You're so insecure you won't even compete. How do

you know you couldn't win, Audrey? You probably could have kept Garth if you'd let his loins shudder a little. Mind you, I'm glad you didn't. Losing once doesn't brand you forever. Garth's not the only guy in the world—he's not even the best. You only think so because Helen managed to lure him away from you."

I lifted my head and sniffed. "I don't know what Jerome told you, but if you think Garth Schuyler ever meant anything to me, you're nuts."

"So how come your hands are clenched into fists? How come in all the time we've spent together, you never once mentioned you have a sister?"

"I didn't mention lots of things!"

"There's no point sticking your head in the sand."

I slowly unclenched my fists, but my stomach was still a hard knot of anger—against Helen, for Garth; against Brad, for bringing the subject up; against Jerome, for blabbing my secrets. And most of all, against me, for being me. "I don't have to listen to this rot."

"Nobody's forcing you to stay."

"Fine, I can take a hint. I'll go." I struggled up from the low sofa.

Brad got up and took a step toward me. With one last mutual glare, we parted. *I'm crazy. I must be crazy, walking out on this man*, a small voice whispered, but my pace didn't slacken as I hurried over the thick carpet. Till I got to the marble hallway, I didn't realize Brad was following me. The carpet cushioned his footfalls, but they suddenly echoed on the hard surface. And still I didn't stop, or even slow down. I wanted to get out before I burst into tears.

"You forgot your purse," he said.

"Thank you."

He pushed it angrily into my hands. It was the last chance, quite possibly the last time I'd see Brad O'Malley.

Common courtesy, if nothing else, demanded some acknowledgment of his help, and some thanks.

"Thanks for—everything," I said vaguely. A quick peek at his face showed it was set in harsh lines. "Thanks" sounded woefully inadequate; I didn't want to leave on such a weak note. Why was I mad anyway? Because he was trying to help, and in the process had unearthed the real me, a bundle of insecurities. He'd discovered my shriveled ego, my smashed heart—the reason I had bowed out of the contest of life, and was content to hide in the woods and write somebody else's story. Everybody knows you can't be cured till you acknowledge you're sick. But I was getting somewhat better. The memory of Garth had faded during the time at Simcoe's cottage. I had finally met someone who outshone him, and now I'd alienated him, too.

"It's generous of you not to do the book on Rosalie," I said. My voice had a ragged, uncertain edge to it.

His harsh face softened almost imperceptibly, but it softened. A faint suggestion of a glow, no more than a glimmer, entered his bleak eyes.

"It's nothing."

"Don't be so modest. It's very generous."

"It's literally nothing," he insisted.

He meant *virtually* nothing, but this wasn't the time for a contest of words. "Thanks for nothing then," I said with a shaky laugh. Even that sounded graceless, and ironic.

A smile so small it was nearly nonexistent flashed across his face, lingering in his eyes. "It's been fun knowing you, Audrey. I still feel I know you, even if I've turned into a stranger. Why did you say that?" he asked softly.

Over his shoulder, Zeus scowled at me. "It must be the company you keep. Picasso, Zeus—those guys."

"I'm exactly the same person I was at the cottage. I feel the same way," he said, not defensively, just stating a fact.

"I feel the same way about you," he added, to make it perfectly clear.

My lower lip moved, but no sound came out. While I stood, hopefully waiting to be rescued, he spoke on. "Audrey, this is ridiculous. Are we really arguing about a set of rooms—about rags and stone and sticks of wood?"

"It's not that—it's the whole way of life." How could I begin to explain my unsuitedness for competing with Hume Mason—*was* he Hume Mason?— and Rosalie Wildewood, and their glitzy set? He'd only say life wasn't a competition, but for me it was. Was he clever enough to explain away a life-style?

"You mean the stuff I write," he said. "I shouldn't have pretended I was an intellectual heavyweight. I only did it to impress you. Not that you were impressed."

"Intellectual pretension is one of my dislikes," I admitted modestly.

"How do you keep track of them all? What *do* you like, anyway?" Anger tinged his voice again, turning me into a block of stone. He gritted his teeth, mentally biting the bullet, and said, "It's the age thing, isn't it?"

I blinked in confusion, "What age thing?"

"The fact that I'm an aging man, and you're still a kid. Oh, I've seen you staring at my wrinkles, laughing at me. I didn't realize the extent of the difference till I saw you and Jerome together. I felt like his father."

"This is crazy . . . How old *are* you, anyway?"

"Nearly forty. I turned thirty-nine last month," he said aggressively, "and I have the arthritis to prove it."

"Really!" I could hardly believe it. Yet I'd taken him for thirty-six or -seven. Two years didn't make that much difference. It was his saying "nearly forty" that threw me.

On his face I read regret that he'd confessed, since I hadn't suspected. "Really. The next one's the big four-O."

"Life begins at forty."

"It's about time. How old are *you*?" He examined me more minutely than felt comfortable.

"Nearly thirty."

"That old?"

This was entirely the wrong response. I should have said twenty-eight. "Didn't Jerome tell you?"

"I was afraid to ask."

"Now we both know the awful truth. Well, I'd better go."

"No, stay. Ten years isn't that big a difference."

"Eleven, actually."

"Let's slug it out. This is worth investigating—it isn't a hopeless case by any means. You're neurotic and prickly and a sl—not one of the world's great housekeepers. I'm old, even-tempered, thick-skinned, and obsessively neat. An odd couple, but complementary. And we *do* have a few things in common. At least we're both in the same business."

Hope and joy trembled through me, then I opened my mouth and said, "I don't see why we can't be friends." I wanted to kick myself. To make it even worse, I added, "I always liked visiting art galleries, and it's not as though I'd have to live here, with the gilt frames." Brad didn't bat an eye, but a little flash told me he had in mind more than visits, possibly even some sharing of accommodations.

"It's a big apartment—two bedrooms," he mentioned, in a voice I couldn't put a description on. Sort of diffident.

Some demon of self-destruction possessed me. "Plenty of room for your ego to swell."

His jaw muscle quivered. "You're doing it again, Audrey."

I hunched my shoulders and gave a watery, apologetic

smile. "Prickly, that's me. Since you picked Jerome's brains last night, you must know they called me the porcupine in college."

"You've changed since college. You were more competitive then."

Changed for the worse, then. "I still am, but more discriminating. I only compete for things that matter to me now."

"Don't *I* matter to you?"

He looked angry, but I think he was only trying to hide the hurt of rejection. I'm prickly, but I'm not mean. I really hate hurting people. "Like I said, we can be friends."

"Good friends, I hope?"

"Bosom pals."

"My favorite kind." He smiled hopefully, and reached for me.

I automatically took a step back, and regretted it before my foot hit the floor. He advanced another pace—thank God. We were within touching distance, within close eye-contact distance. I could sense the attraction between us like a palpable thing. He was going to kiss me, and I wasn't going to try to stop him, not even if I had to get a hammerlock on my tongue. When his hand touched mine, I didn't draw back. I reached for him. My purse slid to the floor, but we both ignored it. We were too involved with other sensations. He pulled me into a crushing embrace. His lips scorched mine, and his hands began a ballet trying in vain to find an entrance through my one-piece dress. When this failed, he began backing into the apartment. At the edge of the rug, he tripped.

"Any special reason why you've suddenly gone into reverse?" I asked. As if I didn't know the destination. Two bedrooms, he'd said.

"What am I going to do with you?" he asked, eyes steaming.

"Succumb to my heaving bosom?"

He went into park, just at the edge of the rug. "Were you really going to walk out on me?" he asked.

"I planned to throw myself under the first passing car, to cause you eternal remorse."

"A sadist! I should have known it when you hit me with the hammer."

"I am what I am."

"I like what you are," he growled, and began examining my physique by hand. Up over my hips, reaching for my breasts, where his hands lingered before lowering to the depression of my waist, the curve of hips. "What is this, a modern chastity gown?"

A knot hardened in my stomach; then a thrill shivered up my spine and down my thighs as he discovered the zipper at the back and slid it down. If women have loins, mine were shuddering. His hands were on my flesh, lowering the sleeves, while his lips nuzzled my ear. Hot lava flowed along my veins.

"Isn't this better than being run over by a car?" he murmured.

"I prefer the Mack truck all right."

As the dress slid to my waist, the intercom buzzed.

"That must be the other paintings!" he said, and ran to the door, while I pulled my dress back on, feeling like a damned fool.

Brad came back with four large parcels, each wrapped in brown paper. "Is there a note?" I asked.

"Yes." He was already opening it. I noticed a tinge of pink starting at his ears and flushing his cheeks as he read.

"What is it? What does it say?"

He gave me a long, wary look before he handed the note to me.

I read:

Brad: I'm sure these will mean a great deal to you. Rosalie would have wanted you to have something to remember her by. I'm joining my mother at Hartland as soon as I can wind down the business here. Do you have any objection to our turning it into a tasteful museum in memory of Rosalie?

> *Sincerely,*
> *Drew Taylor.*

"I don't get it. Why would Rosalie want you to have her things?"

"It's not unusual for parents to leave something to their children," he explained uncertainly.

"She left Lorraine the house. Drew will get it . . ." I looked at the note again. "'I'm joining my *mother* at Hartland.' Drew is really Lorraine's daughter."

"She is. Rosalie didn't have a daughter. She had a son."

It took about thirty seconds for it to sink in. "You! You're her son!" I stared blankly, trying to make sense of it, trying to read any resemblance between them. "It's impossible. You don't look a thing like her."

"I take after my dad. Rosalie left him a month or so after I was born."

"I think we'd better sit down. This is going to be a long story, isn't it?"

"Not really. You were right that she had a child in Europe when she went there to dry out. It was my father's clinic she went to. He was her doctor. Naturally he fell head over heels in love with her," he said, settling on the sofa. "Being an old-fashioned kind of guy, he asked her to marry him, and being temporarily in love with her doctor, she accepted. I'm the result, but a marriage, and especially having a child, didn't jibe with her career plans. I think Dad was sorry he'd ever met her, and was more than willing to keep it hushed up. They got a divorce; she went on to the next husband, and I was raised by my father."

"Have you always known?"

"Till I went to university, I thought my mother was dead. Only a few people at the clinic knew the truth, and they never broadcast it. The story given to lesser friends and relatives was that my father had secretly married an Englishwoman, who died in childbirth. A proud race, the Irish. He wouldn't want to admit to the world he'd made a thundering jackass of himself over an actress. They're just one step above the devil, you know, back home. Dad's done well—remarried years ago."

"He's never admitted all these years that he married Rosalie?"

"He admitted it to me when I was a grown man, by way of warning me to watch out for myself in wicked Dublin. He's up for a knighthood at the moment, which is why he was worried to hear Rosalie's life story was being done. I mentioned it to him on the phone. He asked me to see if I could get his part in her life hushed up. I thought tackling her in person was the best way to go about it. Long-lost son, tears and jubilation, all that sentimental stuff. Rosalie didn't have a sentimental bone in her body. She was coy—said she hadn't told about Dad, but she thought you were suspicious."

"And that's why you followed me to Simcoe's cottage—to see what I was writing about your father."

"To prevent you from writing about him."

"I see. Here I thought it was innocent plagiarism, and all the time you meant to stop me completely. I seem to have an infinite capacity for underestimating you."

"All I found was the bit about gaining weight, so I slivered it out."

"You're not writing an article on her then?"

"No."

"But—and you're really not Hume Mason?"

"Definitely not," he said, offended. "Hume Mason's a woman, Audrey. Nice old gal. I've met her at Belton's a couple of times."

"Then who are you? And what have you got to do with Belton anyway? What were you writing? And where did you get all the money for this museum?" He looked embarrassed. "Madison Gantry!" I exclaimed, and laughed. "I thought so when you made the spaghetti Caruso. You are he, aren't you? You had all his books at the cottage. Gosh, it's better than being Hume Mason, Brad."

"I tried to tell you I wasn't Hume Mason. You refused to believe it, so I left it at that. I needed some excuse for wanting the diaries."

"I would have believed you were Gantry—you could have opened that box of books and proved it. What did you do with them? What is your latest book?"

He gave me a very strange look. I hadn't seen that wary light in his eyes since the first time he came to my cottage. "I'll show you," he said, and went to the office. When he came back, the box had been cut open. He held it out for my inspection. I stared at twenty pink-and-gold copies of *Love's Last Longing.*

"I don't get it. They sent you the wrong books?"

"Unh-unh." His face was crimson.

"But these are Rosalie Wildewood's . . . Oh, my God! Brad, you're not . . . I saw her on TV. She's a gorgeous redheaded dingbat . . . She phoned you."

The crimson face deepened to beet red. "That was my front woman. She takes the rap in public—does the talk shows, goes to conventions. She's also a very good research assistant."

"You're Rosalie Wildewood? It can't be true."

"I used Mom's first name, since it's romantic. Dad's sanatorium in Ireland is called Wildewood. It's in Northern Island actually, on Lough Neagh. I changed the location where I was born when I was talking to Drew, as I was afraid she'd recognize the area. I was always interested in history. There's a lot of interesting history in the Wildewood books."

I couldn't suppress a snort, and didn't try very hard. "Sandwiches of sex and history, but millions of people wouldn't buy the dry bread."

He pokered up. "Gourmets like a little spice. You said you *liked* Rosalie Wildewood."

"No, you idiot. I love her!" In my excitement, I planted a loud smack on his cheek. "You must admit it is kind of funny, Brad."

"That's why I hire Bonnie to do the PR stuff."

First I stopped laughing, then my smile faded. "It was kind of you to agree not to write Roalie's biography."

"I told you it was nothing—literally nothing."

"Nothing my eye! Mason's probably three-quarters finished by now." I jumped up, panic striking my soul.

He pulled me back down. "She's not doing it. She couldn't rake up much scandal, with Rosalie's chums all dead and buried. I met her in California at the funeral—she went to research it. I convinced her you had a gold mine with the diaries, and she couldn't hope to compete. She's doing Fatty Arbuckle instead. A nice, juicy, scandalous life to work with, and lots of public documentation. Fatty's life was better—I guess I mean worse—than Rosalie's."

"That's why you had her picture by your bed," I said, touched at the thought.

"She gave it to me. She asked if Dad needed money, too. I knew she wanted to leave Hartland to Lorraine, and Dad's fine financially, so we're not in the will. His secret would have been blown sky high if we had been. Will you reveal us?"

"It'll come out some time, but I have plenty to work with, without that."

"Thanks. That silly knighthood means a lot to Dad."

"Then it's not silly to him."

"I'll be going over for the ceremony. Care to come with me?"

"I'd like to, but I have to finish my book."

"I can help. No, I'm not talking about ruining it with symbolism. I mean you could use my word processor. It saves a lot of time, Audrey. You've got to get one. And we could work right here, in the museum," he tempted.

My fingers were itching to get at it. "Won't you need it yourself?"

"It looks like I'll be busy redoing the apartment. What is it you hate most, or is it the overall impression of greed and ambition that turned you off?" He looked around at his material possessions. "The statue, the Renoir, the Dürer sketch . . ."

"Don't change the hare for me, Brad," I said. "I identified with that poor trembling creature, all alone with the modern art. I love it all. Really I do. I was just—not jealous exactly—intimidated by your success, I guess."

"I don't see why you should have been intimidated by an old hack writer."

"No, I was jealous of him—her?" He scowled. "I love your wrinkles. They were the first thing I liked about you. The professor scared me a little. What does 'prelapsarian' mean anyway?"

"It's just a critic's word for innocent—before the fall. Of Adam and Eve, I mean. Critics are a little like psychologists: they use big words to puff up small thoughts. Hacks like Mason and Wildewood use understandable words."

"Rosalie Wildewood is not a hack!" I said firmly. Then I stopped and thought. I was boosting someone else's confidence. That wasn't my job. That was the role of successful people, like Brad. "Hume Mason is a hack," I said. "Well-written historical romance can have class. Look at M. M. Kaye, *The Far Pavilions*."

Brad looked at me and smiled ruefully. "Look at us, apologizing for using the talents we have. Let the longhairs write for each other. We'll write for the rest of the world, the real people that want all the lowdown on crime and sex and sin. You'll see Wildewood's style pick up, now that he has a great bosom to watch heave. Come on, I'll introduce you to the word processor."

"I've never used one before. I'm scared stiff."

"I'll be gentle with you." He smiled suggestively. "The sooner you finish with Rosalie Hart, the sooner you can start on her son."

"I should have guessed. I knew all along you were half actor."

"The other half knows how to please a woman. Remember the emperor and the prince?"

"Does either half know how to make coffee? I have work to do. And where's our phone? I have to call my sister in Greece."